D1716735

Murder on Pine Island Bayou

George W. Barclay, Jr.

toExcel

San Jose New York Lincoln Shanghai

Murder on Pine Island Bayou

This edition published by toExcel Press,
an imprint of iUniverse.com, Inc.

For information address:
iUniverse.com, Inc.
620 North 48th Street
Suite 201
Lincoln, NE 68504-3467
www.iUniverse.com

ISBN: 0-595-00031-2

Chapter 1

Batson, Texas
4 P.M. November 17, 1989

The grim-faced hunter slowed down and came to a stop at the only red light. Through narrow eyelids he looked around menacingly. He turned right and pressed on the accelerator. The twin tail pipes roared in response as he drove through the old town. After two miles he again slowed as the concrete pavement ended at a cattle guard, which joined it to the ancient, part shell, part dirt road that snaked its way through deep ruts and holes in the old oil field. The road came to a fork, with one arm running northeast and the other arm to the southeast. Christmas trees, pumping wells, and tank batteries extended in three directions to a distant wood line, marking the separation of the old field from the new.

The hunter turned north and passed through the remainder of the old field until he came to the wood line. The road again forked, with a dirt road to the north and a much-traveled shell road to the east. He hesitated, then drove slowly north on the dirt road. He passed over an old wooden bridge and came to a stop at a gate in the five-strand barbed wire fence that blocked the road. A large sign was clearly visible:

NO TRESPASSING
AMERICAN EASTEX OIL COMPANY

The hunter pulled over to the side of the road and

1

stopped. He removed his automatic shotgun from its rack. He quietly closed the door of his pickup and walked over to the fence. He stepped through it and walked up the road to where it curved back to the west. Following the tree line, he slipped past a warehouse until he could see a white mobile home sitting on stationary blocks. The door was open and through the screen he could see a light and evidence of movement. There was music and laughter. A pickup was parked a few yards away, parallel to the road.

He quietly walked to the door unnoticed. He pointed the shotgun straight ahead from the hip. He bounded up the steps, burst through the unlocked screen door, and screamed with rage as he fired.

Taylor Boudreaux was seated at the table facing the door, and Terry Yberri was seated across the table from him and slightly to his left as the hunter came through the door. Taylor received the first shot in the center of his chest and died instantly. Terry Yberri screamed and, trying to rise, turned toward the gunman. The second blast severed her right hand and tore off the front of her head, killing her instantly.

The hunter carefully pressed the safety. He watched his victims until all movement ceased. He pulled the screen door open with the shotgun, and placing the gun on his shoulder, he calmly walked back to his pickup.

He drove slowly back through the oil field. As he turned on the main road heading toward Old Town, he saw an elderly man walking along the road. The man wore dark glasses and was using a cane to touch the ground in front of him. He was obviously blind. From the bag hanging from his shoulders, it appeared that he was out collecting discarded aluminum cans. The hunter slowed to a stop and watched the old man. After deciding

2

the old man really was blind, the hunter drove off toward the traffic light from which he originally came. He drove straight through the green light and headed south to Raywood. He turned left on U.S. 90, and at Devers he stopped for gasoline.

After paying for his gasoline, he took his change and stepped outside the little convenience store. He located the public phone and looked up the sheriff's number inside the cover of the phone book. He placed coins in the slot and waited.

"Liberty County Sheriff's Office, Dispatcher Grimes speaking," came a voice.

"I have just shot my wife. She is on the old road north of Batson Oil Field," said the hunter, after which he hung up.

The hunter then got into his pickup and headed east on U.S. 90.

Chapter 2

Houston, Texas
3 P.M., November 24, 1989

"I can't take your cash as a retainer, Mr. Fuentes," said Sandra Lerner, considerably annoyed. "You take that suitcase full of hundred dollar bills to a bank and deposit it. Then you write me a check, and if it doesn't bounce, I might consider hearing your cousin's case—maybe," said Sandra as she lit a little cigar and smoked defiantly.

"Si, señora, I think that can be arranged," replied Mr. Fuentes, smiling. "Where freedom at stake money is no objection." Mr. Fuentes was a handsome Latino, with his styled hair, closely trimmed mustache, $600 suit, gold cuff links, manicured nails, and highly polished shoes. "My cousin will be very happy you take his case." He picked up his suitcase as he rose and started for the door.

"Mr. Fuentes, your cousin is a rat! But in North America we believe that even human rats deserve a fair trial and a good defense—whether they can pay or not. If you can't pass that money on to some unsuspecting bank teller, the state will pay to provide your cousin with a public defender."

"I know, Miss Lerner, but my cousin, he wants you," answered Mr. Fuentes as he very graciously excused himself, suitcase in hand.

"Miss Lerner," called a voice from the intercom.

Sandra pushed a button and answered, "Yes, Betty."

"You have a long distance call. A Mr. Scott Mac-Wright, from the law firm of MacWright, MacWright, and

4

MacWright of Beaumont, Texas. Shall I put him through or take his number?"

"Put Scotty through, Betty, and try not to interrupt us. He's an old boyfriend of mine from decades past. Maybe he is free and wants a date."

"Right," came a quick reply.

Sandra smoked her cigar and waited.

"Sandra?"

"Yes, Scotty?"

"I need you to help me."

"At last you've come to your senses, Scotty."

"It's business, Sandra. Murder."

"Oh hell, Scott, you want me to kill somebody or get you out of jail?"

"Neither. I want you to help me defend a client who is in jail waiting to be tried for Murder One," replied Mr. MacWright slowly.

"I can't, Scotty. There's no way I can get away from here until after Christmas, too many irons in the fire."

"We start picking the jury December twenty-sixth, and the trial starts January second up in Woodville."

"Woodville! Where's Woodville?" asked Sandra.

"About fifty miles north of Beaumont. It's in Tyler County. The Hardin County Jail was full, and the district courts in Jefferson County have a two-year backlog. Our client is in a private cell in the Tyler County Jail. The district attorney has jurisdiction over Hardin and Tyler counties, and the district judge has jurisdiction over Tyler and Jasper counties, so we all agreed to a change in venue from Hardin County to Tyler County. Woodville is the county seat."

"Scotty, you've gotten me thoroughly confused. The murder occurred in Hardin County, I guess? Maybe you

5

had better brief me on the details, so I can get it straight in my mind."

"Murders, Sandra, plural, two murders. Our client— 'Captain' Gilbert Alfred Yberri, sixty-four years, white, millionaire landowner, oil man, Korean War hero, and eccentric—is accused of murdering his wife and her lover in her boyfriend's mobile home out in the woods north of the old Batson oil field around four P.M. on November seventeenth. The motive was jealousy, the means was a twelve-gauge shotgun, and the opportunity existed in that Captain Yberri claims he was on a deer stand, about eight miles away, from two P.M. until six P.M., with no witness to verify his whereabouts."

"My God, Scotty, you mean he has no alibi?" replied Sandra.

"That's right. And furthermore, the spent shells found at the murder scene are the same brand as those in his hunting vest, his palm and fingerprints were on the gate leading to the mobile home, and the Liberty County sheriff received an anonymous phone call around four forty-five P.M. from Devers, Texas, from a man admitting to have shot his wife north of the old Batson oil field."

"Liberty County! My God, Scotty, that's the fifth county you've mentioned. I'm going to have to get out my map just to keep the counties straight. Up until ten minutes ago I thought that Harris County was the only place with big-time crime."

"Batson is in west Hardin County, about ten miles from the Liberty County line. It's easily confused," replied Scott.

"Not if you've lived your entire life in Hardin County. What did the Hardin County sheriff say to that?"

"He thinks Captain Yberri deliberately drove to

6

Devers to make the call to draw them off the track," replied Scott.

"Oh," replied Sandra. "Why do they call him captain, and what kind of war hero?"

"He got a battlefield commission in Korea and came home a captain. He was awarded the Distinguished Service Cross for single-handedly holding a hill against a battalion of North Korean infantry with a Browning automatic rifle. They found thirty-five bodies he had killed stacked up in the mouth of a ravine. When he ran out of ammunition, he called friendly artillery fire in on his own position and then killed two more with a bayonet in hand-to-hand combat. When reinforcements arrived, he was the only survivor of his platoon. He probably would have been awarded the Medal of Honor, except he lived to tell the story and there were no eyewitnesses."

"Well, he's going to need an eyewitness to get out of these murders, and we can't use his war record in our defense either. It's too bloody. What did Captain Yberri say happened?" asked Sandra.

"When he came home from hunting, his wife was gone. He called over to his daughter's and then went out and looked for her. He called the Hardin County sheriff and reported her missing. That's when the sheriff and his deputies had the gate unlocked and found the bodies. The rest will be in the investigating officer's and medical examiner's reports, which have not been finalized. I'll send you copies as soon as I get them," replied Scott.

"Look, Scotty, I take it you've got a wife and a houseful of kids and possibly a grandchild or two?" asked Sandra.

"That's right, and they are all going to be at my house for the holidays," replied Scott.

"Look, you go ahead and sign me in as co-counsel of

7

record, handle the jury selection yourself, and I'll drive to Beaumont on Saturday, December thirtieth. I'll check into the Holiday Inn on Walden Road and spend the night. I'll call you at eight A.M. on Sunday morning, and we can spend the next two days interviewing witnesses and planning our defense."

"That sounds good to me, Sandra. It's a tremendous relief to have you," replied Scott.

"Have you got any ideas on how to defend Captain Yberri? The circumstantial evidence is pretty strong," said Sandra, quietly.

"*Whitlock versus the State of Texas*, Beaumont, Texas, nineteen-forty-eight," replied Scott.

"Obviously that was a local case in which the accused was acquitted of murder. Briefly tell me the details, please," replied Sandra.

"Whitlock shot his wife's lover and accidentally shot his wife while they were embracing. The jury decided he shot the lover to defend his home and his wife was killed accidentally when she stepped into the field of fire. He was acquitted on both charges," replied Scott.

"Hm-m! We'd better not count on it. That was forty years ago. I'm not even sure you could get a case of adultery before a judge in nineteen-ninety. We'd better go for reasonable doubt, which will require a lot of investigative work for you and me before that trial starts. You make me a list of prospective witnesses, and we will start interviewing them on Sunday morning."

"Sounds good, Sandra. I'm happy to be working with you again. Like old times, huh?"

"Like, old times, Scotty. See you," said Sandra, as she slowly put down the phone.

"Bye," said Scotty MacWright.

Chapter 3

Beaumont, Texas
4 P.M., December 30, 1989
Beaumont is a nice town, thought Sandra. *The traffic isn't hectic like in Houston. It has modern conveniences, local color, and you can drive anywhere in town in ten minutes.*

She pulled into the parking lot of the Beaumont Plaza Holiday Inn. It was about half full. *No conventions,* thought Sandra. As she followed the bell captain into the lobby she noticed the large dining room was half full. Things seemed quiet enough. She reserved her room for a week.

"Are you the only one working tonight?" asked Sandra of the bell captain as she followed him into the elevator.

"Yes, ma'am. Everybody's on holiday," he replied. "Things won't pick up around here until Tuesday, when all the salesmen and manufacturers' reps will be back."

"Where is the action around here on Saturday night?" asked Sandra.

"Well, ma'am, we have a bar downstairs where they'll be watching football on TV and there's the lounge down the hall where they'll have a combo at nine," replied the bell captain.

"I was thinking about going out and taking in the local color and observing the temperament of the populace while they're celebrating," said Sandra.

"Yes, ma'am," said the bell captain, smiling. "There're two popular places close by. Just get up on IH-10

9

and follow it to the right toward Port Arthur. If you get off at the Fannett Road exit, the side road will take you to Phaze II, which is a disco for young people—lots of flashing lights and hard rock music. If you get off on the West Port Arthur road and drive about a mile outside the city limits, you'll see Lou Ann's. It's a big dance hall for grownups. It should be crowded tonight. They have a Cajun band from DeQuincy," replied the bell captain.

"Will they let unescorted females in?" asked Sandra, as she followed him off the elevator and down the brightly lit hallway toward 806.

"Just show them your driver's license, so they'll know you're over twenty-one. The cover charge is five dollars which will be good for about two drinks. If you want more, you have to pay cash."

The bell captain opened the door and flipped on the lights. He placed her bags on the bed, turned on the central heating, and walked over to the TV.

"This TV comes on by pushing this button or by using the remote control by the bed. If you want to watch pay TV, you turn on channel three and turn this knob here. The movie selections are displayed on top," said the bell captain, as he held out his hand.

Sandra tipped him a dollar and read the movie selections: Red October, Presumed Innocent, The Verdict, and Debbie Does Dallas.

"My God," said Sandra, "maybe I'd better watch TV rather than going out to Lou Ann's; however, it's cheaper at Lou Ann's, if you only have two drinks."

Chapter 4

Lou Ann's was not hard to find. It looked like a large barn, and the neon sign showed from a distance. There were about a thousand cars parked around it, and Sandra could hear the music. Its entrance was a small doorway that opened to a short hallway at the end of which sat a costumed ticket clerk. The noise was deafening.

The clerk took Sandra's driver's license and $5 bill and stamped her on the back of the hand. As she walked into the huge crowded room, she saw a deputy leaning against the wall. He wore a nightstick on one side and a holstered service pistol on the other. His eyes were following her.

Sandra looked around the room. It was huge. The crowd was boisterous, and the dance floor was packed. They seemed to be performing a strange waltz to a beat she had never heard before. There were many tables, all taken, and it was difficult to find empty chairs in the darkened room. The band was loud.

The deputy walked up to her side. He was black, six foot four, and weighed about two hundred and forty pounds.

"Would madam prefer a seat at the bar, or is she looking for her party?" asked the deputy.

Sandra was startled by his powerful baritone voice and perfect English. He could have been the Prince of Wales, but he sounded more English, with just a touch of a French accent. She guessed Jamaica, but wasn't quite sure.

11

"No, I'm alone, and I prefer a table close to the dance floor, so I can watch," said Sandra.

"I think we can manage those accommodations. Just follow me, please," said the deputy, as he made his way through the crowd.

Sandra followed closely behind the large officer until he led her to a table that was empty and surrounded by six vacant metal, folding chairs. He walked to the chair giving the best view of the dance floor and gently pulled it back from the table; while holding the back, he motioned Sandra to be seated.

"Thank you," said Sandra, sincerely. "Please be seated for a moment. I have this intense curiosity to know where you were born."

"Just for a moment, madam," replied the officer, as he took a seat two chairs over. "I have a similar question to ask you."

My goodness, thought Sandra, *he knows I'm a stranger.* She had dressed in medium heels, blue jeans, and a T-shirt with the message Eat More Armadillo, fluffed her hair, and put on dark red lipstick and plenty of rouge. She thought she was in style with the local dress. She wanted to blend in with the crowd. She looked around, and the women seemed to be dressed the same, except perhaps crayfish and alligator were more popular fare than armadillo. Oh well, she knew the armadillo came from Texas; she had seen pictures of them. Out in west Texas it was jackrabbits.

"I'll go first," said Sandra. "You're from Bermuda?"

"Wrong," replied the officer, "and you're an undercover officer with the DEA or the Liquor Control Board?"

"Wrong!" said Sandra. "I'm a lawyer from Houston, staying at the Holiday Plaza."

"I'm a naturalized citizen, born and raised in

12

Dominica, a little island off Venezuela, and I'm a deputy sheriff on duty."

They both laughed.

"Tell me how you knew I was a stranger. I'm dressed just like all these other women," said Sandra.

"Easy to the experienced observer, madam. If you will observe these other ladies walk or dance, you see that their weight is totally on the foot touching the floor. When they place the other foot forward or backward as they dance, they shift their weight totally to the foot touching the floor while lifting the other foot. It gives a slight exaggeration of the hip movement. It is an unconscious effort on their part, acquired from many years of dancing."

"Fantastic!" exclaimed Sandra. "Does everybody on Dominica speak perfect English?"

"Yes, madam, we have known only Elizabethan English for three hundred years, since the English brought my forefathers from Africa to work on the sugar-cane plantations. We were given our freedom in eighteen-thirty-four, which was thirty years before the slaves were freed in North America and fifty-four years before they were freed in Brazil," replied the deputy proudly.

"How interesting," said Sandra. "You've taught me how to walk and given me an unforgettable history lesson all in a brief conversation. Ah, look, there are two couples coming through the door and pointing toward this table. I'm going to have guests."

The officer rose from his chair and placed it against the table. He bent over and whispered to Sandra just before he departed. "Watch out for that tall, dark, oil field roughneck with the mustache on the left. That's Jacques

13

LaShute, and he can be a mean Frenchman when he gets a few drinks."

"Thanks," replied Sandra. She watched the couples as they approached her table. It was obvious she was going to have company. They seemed to be well on their way to celebrating New Year's Eve early. The men helped their women, presumably their wives, into chairs at her side, leaving one chair empty next to the dance floor. Sandra met the gaze of each of the women and nodded in greeting. The men were looking around the room for their friends.

"I can take your order now," said a waitress, standing at Sandra's side.

"I'll have a Miller Lite," said Sandra. The waitress made a mental note and then took the orders of the two couples. The women ordered beer, and the men ordered Jack Daniels with beer chasers. She disappeared as quickly as she had appeared and came back in a few minutes with their drinks.

The band began to play a lively number, and the crowd cheered and clapped in response. Jacques La-Shute belted down his Jack Daniels and headed toward Sandra. Sandra was petrified with fear and indecision.

"Come on, little gal, let's dance this while it's hot," said Jacques, as he firmly took hold of Sandra's wrist and helped her to her feet.

Sandra opened her mouth, but words would not come. She was speechless as she followed him out to the dance floor. When they joined the dancers, he forced his way through the couples until he found about a foot of dancing space. He turned, bent over, and put his arm around Sandra's back, his left hand grasping hers tightly. Sandra did the best she could, but every step backward resulted in a collision with another couple. Jacques was

14

feeling great. He let out a loud whoop and said in French: *"Laissez les bons temps rouler."*

He gave her a big squeeze, and Sandra felt one of her ribs give. It took away her breath. Mercifully, the music stopped. The couples headed back to their tables, and the orchestra took a much-deserved break. Jacques kept a firm grip on Sandra as she followed him toward his table.

As they neared the table, Sandra could see Jacques's friend standing behind the chair of Jacques's beautiful wife. She was holding her long black hair back to expose her ear. Jacques's friend bent over and whispered into her ear or something. Jacques instantly became furious and with no hesitation dropped Sandra's hand. With two long steps, he was at his friend's throat. He drew his fist back threateningly.

"You goddamned coon ass. You make pass at my wife, and I'll kill you." Jacques's eyes were filled with rage, and he appeared quite ready to fulfill his threat.

"Don't, Jacques! Jerry was just letting me smell the perfume you gave her for Christmas. I meant nothing by it." He was gasping for breath as Jacques loosened his grip and let go of his throat.

Jacques turned around and glared at his wife. "I kill you, too, if I see such crap as this going on again."

Sandra saw the deputy approaching their table. She calmly picked up her purse and carefully made her way to the exit. Her ribs hurt her slightly as she breathed. She felt lucky to get out in one piece.

She did not feel safe until she returned to her room in the Holiday Plaza. She double locked her door and turned on the TV. She fell asleep watching Sandy Stern file a motion for dismissal of murder charges against his client, Rusty.

15

Chapter 5

The phone rang at 7 A.M. It was Scotty.

"Hello, Sandra, did I wake you?"

"Hello, Scotty. You surely did, but it is nice to hear your voice. Where are you?"

"Oh, I'm down here in the restaurant waiting for you to join me," he replied.

"Oh dear, it will be a few minutes. What do you think I ought to wear?"

"Outdoor clothes and boots, if you have them. We will probably walk around in the oil field and woods some. They don't know about sidewalks and modern plumbing where we're going."

"I'll wear cowboy boots, jeans, and a blue denim jacket. Is that alright?"

"That's fine, Sandra. I can hardly wait to see you."

"What kind of vehicle are you driving, Scotty?"

"A Jeep Wagoneer with four-wheel drive and mud tires."

"Sounds like rugged country where we're going."

"Right. Come on down. We can chat while we're eating."

Sandra showered and was ready in twenty minutes. Scott met her at the elevator, and they embraced like the old friends they were.

"Sandra, you don't look a day older. You are still trim and as beautiful as ever."

"It's because I'm still barren, Scotty. You passed up

16

your chance to make an honest woman out of me. You look a little more 'mature.' Hopefully, you are wiser."

"Now, Sandra, you know there can be only one chief in a tepee. Charlotte just stays home and housewifes. Bless her. Every man should have one."

"You are a male chauvinist, Scott MacWright. Now that we've completed that little discussion again for the umpteenth time, let's eat breakfast. I'm famished."

Sandra ordered ham and two eggs. Scott ordered dry toast and oatmeal. They both had black coffee.

"Looks like you are watching your cholesterol, Scotty," teased Sandra. "You jogging, too?"

"Three miles every day but Sunday," answered Scotty, smiling. "I want to outlive my dad."

"What happened to your dad?"

"Oh, he retired and is living in a house on Toledo Bend Reservoir with my new stepmother. Fishing every day."

"Aha! How old is your step-mother, Scotty?" laughed Sandra.

"She's about fifteen years younger than I am. Energetic and pretty. They're thinking about starting a family."

Sandra laughed. Scotty blushed.

"Sandra, I don't quite know where to begin on this case. It could be very simple if he is guilty and very complicated if he is telling the truth. I've got copies of all the reports in a briefcase in my Jeep. You can have them to keep when we get back. I've got a list of possible suspects, too."

"Pictures of the murder scene?"

"They're in the briefcase."

"Did the autopsy provide anything surprising?"

"Yes and no! Taylor Boudreaux had a hole through

17

the middle of his chest. He was facing the killer. Terry Yberri's right hand was blown off along with her face and half her head. Her body fell over his head. The blood alcohol tests were both negative. He had A+ blood type and she had A-."

"What was the surprise?" asked Sandra.

"Terry Yberri had a congenital condition called dextrocardia and situs inversus. Very rare! Maybe one in a million live births. The heart and the great vessels are on the right side of the chest, and all the internal abdominal organs are reversed."

"Hm-m!" said Sandra. "That's a new one on me. It has no effects on growth and development and no effects in later life?"

"That's right. It's just rare, that's all. Usually detected by accident. The heart and all the organs are reversed. Old Dr. Castillo, the pathologist, got real excited. It made his day."

"I bet it did. Ugh! I'd hate to be a forensic pathologist and see all those mutilated bodies come in."

"You bet."

Sandra looked at her watch. "Brief me on the investigating officer's reports so we can take off."

"Well, when the Hardin County Sheriff's Office received the telephone call from the Liberty County Sheriff's Office it was about five P.M. They dispatched a car with two deputies out to investigate. Deputies Black and White. They drove around the back of the oil field. They found the gates to the American Eastex field locked, so they didn't investigate further. A gauger locks them all at five P.M. Then they interviewed two men on deer stands. They had heard shots, but had seen no woman. They interviewed a blind man that lives in an old shack down in the oil field, and naturally, he had seen nothing.

18

They decided the call was a hoax and drove down to Kountze. When Captain Yberri called in at nine P.M. and reported his wife was missing, they drove back to Batson and picked up the gauger, Alfred Gange, and opened the gate blocking the road to Taylor Boudreaux's mobile home. Then they found the bodies of the victims. Alfred Gange and Captain Yberri made positive identifications of the bodies. The sheriff and the justice of the peace came out. They had a homicide specialist and photographer from Jefferson County come out, take pictures, and dust everything, including the gate, for fingerprints. The bodies were transported to Beaumont for autopsy. They read Captain Yberri his rights, and he called me in as his lawyer. I called you, and here we are. Let's go to Batson."

"Let's go," said Sandra, jumping up.

Chapter 6

Scotty drove west on Walden and turned north on Major Drive, bypassing the city. He drove to 105 and again turned east. As he crossed over Pine Island Bayou he explained to Sandra, "Pine Island Bayou separates Jefferson County from Hardin County. Batson is twenty miles to the west. The next town is Sour Lake." Sandra took it all in. When Scotty reached within three miles of the junction of Texas 105 and FM RD 770 he stopped his Jeep.

"See that old hard top road angling off to the right? That's the old Sour Lake to Batson Road. About two miles down that old road is where Captain Yberri has his deer stand. It's about three hundred yards off the road," explained Scotty.

"Does anybody travel that road, Scotty? It looks pretty rough."

"Just Hosea Lopez, the Mexican that feeds old man Havaard's cows."

"What time does he feed them?"

"Around four-thirty P.M. every day. He dumps hay off the back of a pickup. They only feed them November through March."

"You know, he would have to pass right by Captain Yberri's truck parked on the road."

"Yes, if it were there."

"Have him subpoenaed, Scotty."

"That may be hard to do, Sandra. He's an illegal alien and is difficult to find."

"We've got to find him. He can help us establish reasonable doubt—he may provide the alibi we need."

"I'll try," said Scotty and he drove off slowly. He slowed down again as they turned left of FM RD 770. "That fence over there across the road extends around the entire American Eastex Oil Company field. It runs all the way east to Saratoga and north to Thicket. The fence snakes around the old Batson field to the warehouse where Taylor Boudreaux was shot, then it runs north to Thicket. There are hundreds of producing wells in there. There is plenty of timber, and they run cows in pasture."

"Where is Captain Yberri's land?"

"Ah, it starts about a half a mile from here, where Pine Island Bayou crosses the road, and extends all the way into Old Town and runs over to the AmEastex fence. He owns all of the old oil field. Captain Yberri does not fence his land or cattle. He has about sixty-five active wells on his land, which are leased and operated by LouTex Oil Company. Captain Yberri and his daughter do contract pumping and gauging for LouTex on their own land."

"Scotty how do you know so much about their properties, boundaries, and such?"

"My firm has handled the Yberri estate and their various investments and trust funds for three generations, Sandra. That's why he called me when they put him in jail."

"Scotty, how much is the captain worth? Rough figures."

"Roughly forty or fifty million, Sandra. It's self-perpetuating. I can't tell you really how much. The Yberris are a hardworking and frugal family, as you will soon see."

"Oh! Oh! What's this? Stop! Scotty, there is a big tank

21

truck turning across the road up ahead. There's a man opening the gate, and they are driving onto AmEastex property," said Sandra.

"That would be Alfred Gange, the gauger for Am-Eastex, opening the gate. It looks like the tank truck is owned by Pakco Limited. They must be going in for a load of crude. That's a big truck—three hundred barrels, I'd guess," replied Scotty.

"Is Alfred Gange a suspect?"

"Could be, I guess; he's the one that locks all the gates at five P.M. and doesn't open them until the next morning. He has a home just down the road. He's married to Taylor Boudreaux's former wife, and she has two teenage children from her marriage to Taylor."

"Goodness! Let's subpoena him. Also, why don't we stop and interview his wife?"

"She may be hostile, Sandra. She and Alfred had not spoken to Taylor for several years prior to his death. Taylor refused to pay child support, and Alfred was furious about it."

"Our client's life is at stake, Scotty. We have to try. Maybe she can help."

Scotty remained silent and turned off the road onto the shell drive leading to a beautiful brick home. It was sitting approximately two hundred yards off the road and was surrounded by tall oaks from which Spanish moss hung in uneven rows almost touching the ground. There was a large barn and corral out back. Tractors, trucks, and heavy equipment were visible in the background. Dogs were barking. The barn loft was filled with hay, and various farm animals could be seen feeding in the pasture extending back into the woods.

"This is Alfred Gange's home, Sandra. We had better

both get out and go talk with her. She may close the door on us."

"Goodness! It looks prosperous. I didn't know pumpers and gaugers made that much money."

"Well, Alfred is a hard worker. Not only does he check all the wells for AmEastex, but he and Josh Carpenter own all the cattle pasturing on their property inside the fence I showed you."

"Who is Josh Carpenter?"

"He is the district superintendent for the American Eastex Oil Company. They have an office in Beaumont," answered Scotty.

"Who actually owns the land American Eastex has fenced up?"

"Some of it is owned by AmEastex, but most of it is owned by absentee landowners who are descendants of the original pioneers that settled this area. Most of them live in Houston or Dallas. AmEastex just sends them checks for leasing rights and oil royalties."

"That's the kind of oil person I'd like to be," replied Sandra, smiling. "'The checks are in the mail.'"

Sandra and Scotty got out of the Jeep. Several dogs welcomed them as they walked up the driveway to the large home. They pressed on the doorbell. In a few moments, a tall, slender woman in her early forties opened the door. Mrs. Gange had long black hair. She was attractive but wore no makeup. She was wearing the traditional T-shirt, jeans, and loafers.

"Yes?" asked Mrs. Gange.

"I'm Scotty MacWright and this is Miss Sandra Lerner. We are attorneys defending Captain Yberri."

Mrs. Gange opened the door and forced a smile. She extended an arm and beckoned them in.

"Please come in. You will have to excuse this mess.

23

I don't have a maid. My kids have gone to church, and Alfred is out working. It's just me and the dogs plus all the animals out back."

Sandra quickly surveyed the room and house in turn—wall-to-wall carpet and tile, beautiful furniture, and a large TV sitting next to the fireplace in which there were real logs. Toward the back there was a large den and kitchen combination, and on her right there was a giant dining room with a dining table that would seat eight. The furniture was beautiful and expensive. Mrs. Gange has good taste, thought Sandra, and she didn't see any mess.

"Thank you," replied Scotty as he followed the two ladies into the living room. Sandra and Scott sat on the couch, and Mrs. Gange sat across from them in a padded chair. Obviously, this was a sitting room for guests. There was a much larger TV back in the den. They were getting the formal welcome.

"May I get you folks some coffee? There's some made," said Mrs. Gange.

"Yes! Thanks!" Sandra spoke with enthusiasm. She was eager to get on with it.

"Yes," said Scotty. "Black."

"Yours black, too, Miss Lerner?"

"I'll take just a touch of sugar in mine," said Sandra. "I have a taste for sweet things."

Mrs. Gange smiled a genuine smile, showing beautiful white teeth. "So do I, Miss Lerner. Why don't you all come back in the den and enjoy the view? I'll get us some coffee and cakes, and we can have a nice talk. I don't hardly get any visitors except teenagers and kinfolks."

"That will be nice," said Sandra as they got up to follow her.

The west side of the den was all transparent glass with sliding glass doors that opened onto a large back-yard and provided a wonderful view of the barn, pasture, and woods. Cattle were eating hay by a large water trough, and several deer were eating corn spread on the ground by a nearby feeder. There were ducks, geese, and chickens walking around the barnyard, and she could see a few goats in the pasture. Several hounds were lying around in the sun, seemingly unaroused by it all.

Sandra and Scotty sat on the couch and took it all in. Mrs. Gange set a tray containing coffee cups of real china, a platter of homemade tea cakes, and a small bowl of sugar in front of them. She poured coffee from a Mr. Coffee decanter. They all settled down and looked out the glass wall for a minute.

"I see deer out there," said Scott.

"Those are our pets. Alfred won't let anybody hunt in our pasture. Deer like corn, just as humans relish sweets. They are primarily browsers and won't touch the hay," replied Mrs. Gange.

"Mrs. Gange, may we ask you about the murders of Mrs. Yberri and Mr. Boudreaux?" said Sandra.

"Yes, ma'am," she replied slowly. "You know that Taylor Boudreaux was my ex-husband and father of my two children. Terry Yberri was a good friend, and I will miss her."

"Mrs. Gange, where were you and your husband on the afternoon of the murder?" asked Sandra.

"Alfred finished up the wells and drove through the field locking the gates. He passed by the last gate, which was Taylor's, at five P.M. The gate was already locked, so he kept going. He came directly to the house here. We—Alfred and I—loaded up his pickup with as much hay as we could and took off down the Saratoga road to feed the

25

cows. I was with him until dark. We came back home and fixed supper. They came and got him to open up the gate at nine-thirty P.M."

"Who had reason to shoot the victims, Mrs. Gange?" asked Sandra.

"Terry—I don't know. Lots of people knew Taylor. A few disliked him enough to want him dead. Alfred even threatened to shoot him once or twice, because he refused to pay the child support. He was just joking. About the only thing Alfred will shoot is a fox or wolf that's trying to get our animals. He's not a hunter," replied Mrs. Gange thoughtfully.

"Why did you divorce Taylor Boudreaux?" asked Sandra.

"Two big reasons, Miss Lerner, whiskey and women. Everybody called him Old Taylor, and he would always reply, 'Either.' That was his private joke, but I got tired of it after ten years."

"What was Terry Yberri doing in his mobile home?"

"I don't know, but you can bet your last dollar it wasn't hanky-panky. She just happened to be in the wrong place at the wrong time. Some crazy person shot them, Miss Lerner. Nobody hated Taylor that much," replied Mrs. Gange.

"You don't think the captain shot them in a fit of jealous rage?"

"No ma'am, but he seems to be the only suspect. It was that crazy telephone call that led them to him. He'd have to be crazy to drive all the way over to Liberty County and call in to tell them he shot his wife."

"Who else goes into AmEastex field besides you and Mr. Gange?" asked Sandra.

"Josh Carpenter, the district superintendent, was sitting in his deer stand about a mile across the woods when it happened, and old Antoine Como. Mr. Como is an elderly black man that lives in a shack on the east bank of the fish lake and is employed by Alfred and Mr. Carpenter to help feed the cows. If he wasn't feeding the cows, he was fishing when it happened," answered Mrs. Gange.

"Who had keys to the locks?" asked Sandra.

"Mr. Carpenter, Alfred, and Taylor Boudreaux," answered Mrs. Gange.

"What was Mr. Boudreaux's job with Eastex, Mrs. Gange?"

"He was a tool pusher. He just lived in the old field. AmEastex has about twelve drilling wells, wildcats, scattered out through southeast Texas and southwest Louisiana. Taylor made rounds on all of them and checked on the equipment. He reported directly to Mr. Carpenter."

"How did he get along with Mr. Carpenter?" asked Sandra.

"Okay, I guess. Mr. Carpenter is married to Taylor's sister, and they go back many years. A real brother-in-law arrangement. It's not that Taylor was so bad. He was a very good oil man. But he made it a habit to drop in on the employees' wives while their husbands were working. Some of the men didn't take too kindly to it."

"Thank you, Mrs. Gange," said Scotty.

Scotty and Sandra rose and started to make their departure.

"You're welcome, Mr. MacWright, and you, too, Miss Lerner. You come back sometime when you've got more time, and I will tell you the life history of everybody in west Hardin County. I get lonely out here at times."

"Thank you, Mrs. Gange. May we subpoena you and

your husband, if we decide to call you on the witness stand?" asked Sandra.

"Yes, ma'am. I've always liked the captain, and Terry was my best friend."

Chapter 7

"Scotty, how much money can you clear on a cow raising them out here like they do?" asked Sandra as they got into the Jeep.

"Anywhere from three-fifty to five hundred for a one-year-old, if the market is good," answered Scott. "It depends on a lot of things. The weather here is mild most of the year. They supplement their feeding during the winter months only."

"That's good money. If you pastured a hundred cows, you could clear as much as a lawyer," said Sandra, laughing.

"That's right," said Scott as he backed out of the driveway and headed toward Batson.

"Scotty, don't you smoke?"

"No! but it's okay if you want to light up, Sandra. I'll crack the window."

"No, Scotty, I want you to outlive your father. You've got a young and pretty stepmother, remember."

"Sandra, you don't miss a thing."

"Too bad for you men the U.S. didn't join Utah, instead of the other way around," said Sandra, smiling.

"Sandra, just up ahead where you see all those cars and trucks parked is the Pentecostal church. Directly across is the road to Captain Yberri's home. It runs east into the woods about a quarter of a mile. There's no one there right now. His daughter lives out on the Moss Hill road. We can see her later. She's probably at church anyway," said Scott.

"I'm with you, Scotty," answered Sandra.

Scotty turned right on the shell road running along a wood line. Sandra could hear the singing in the church. It was 11 A.M.

"We'd better make this brief if we are going to interview all the witnesses today. I know when I'm about to get a history lecture. It's my lawyer gut feeling."

"That's right, Sandra, I'm going to show you things you only read about in the history books," replied Scott, smiling proudly.

As they drove slowly toward a clearing in the distance. Sandra began to hear dogs barking. Before they could see the house, a pack of hounds and several mongrels came bounding out of the clearing and stopped in the middle of the road. They were jumping up and down, milling around, and barking in an apparent joyous fashion. It occurred to Sandra that they were expecting the captain or perhaps somebody to feed them. Then she saw the house.

The large, freshly painted white house was strictly turn-of-the-century. There was a front porch that ran the entire width. Sandra guessed it was at least twelve by fifty feet. There were two ancient wooden rocking chairs with cowhide bottoms and an ancient swing. There were six polished log posts spaced across the front. Wash tables were on either end, complete with washbasins and a long handled dipper hung from a nail. There was a shingled roof and a chimney on either end. There was an open hallway that ran down through the center of the house, apparently through which the dogs had come. There was a well out back, as well as a freshly painted outdoor toilet and a large barn. The road ran past the barn and disappeared back into the woods. Sandra jumped out of the Jeep and ran around to the back of the huge old house. She breathed a sigh of relief when she

30

saw an air conditioner in the back bedroom window. She looked around and noticed a septic tank, a butane gas tank, and a water hydrant. She looked up and noticed power lines strung to the house.

"You know Scotty, for a while there I really thought they did have well water and outdoor plumbing," said Sandra.

Scotty was smiling broadly as he watched Sandra marvel at the house. "The old rub board and butter churn are back in the storage room, and the captain didn't throw away the kerosene lamps," he volunteered.

"What year was this built?"

"Captain Yberri's father built it in nineteen-oh-one. They didn't get electricity and indoor plumbing until nineteen-forty-six. That hall down the middle is called the dogtrot, but it was really designed that way to provide air conditioning. If you will notice, the house is facing west. That's so they can all sit on the front porch and watch the sun go down in the evening."

"How quaint, Scotty. Doesn't this make you feel domestic?"

"Get in the Jeep, Sandra. I want to take you down to see his grandfather's old place. It was built in eighteen-seventy. You see those lines? They have put lights in the old place, but it doesn't have running water or indoor plumbing. It's not the oldest house in Hardin County, but it's the best preserved."

They got in the Jeep and followed the old dirt road back into the woods. A buck crossed the road about fifty yards in front of them. It startled Sandra. She looked through the trees and could see squirrels playing. Then she saw it!

"Stop, Scotty. I've got to get out. I see a real live armadillo rooting up the dirt out there. I've never seen a

31

live one before." When she slammed the door, the armadillo looked up, pointed its ears in her direction, and then turned and ran off into the woods. Sandra stopped, disappointed, and got back into the Jeep. Scotty was watching her curiously.

"Sandra, there's thousands of armadillos around here. They root up the grubs and eat the snakes. Armadillo is man's best friend. During the depression instead of a chicken in every pot, out here it was an armadillo in every washpot. They are really quite tasty. They taste like pork. You know, raccoon and possum have sort of a strong, greasy taste, like dog, but an armadillo is good."

"Stop, Scotty, you are making me nauseous. You wouldn't want to eat a cuddly little animal like an armadillo. I bet they would make great pets."

Scott slowed to a halt when the log cabin came in view. It was facing west with a dogtrot through the middle. It was sitting high on an earthen platform, made out of fourteen-inch hewn logs with mud caulking between. There were wooden windows that were bolted on the inside and two well-preserved mud chimneys on either end. The cypress shingled roof extended out and provided a shade in front, but there was no front porch. The front doors were locked.

"Okay, Scotty, I'm impressed. There was never anything in River Oaks like this where I grew up. Let's hear the history lesson now. Remember we are out lawyering, not sightseeing."

They stood outside in the shade and looked at the ancient structure. Both tried to imagine what it was like a hundred years ago.

"Old Captain Yberri was a Russian ship's captain that tried to run the Yankee blockade to buy cotton during the Civil War. His ship was confiscated by the Yankees, but he was put ashore in New Orleans with the entire ship's treasure. Instead of turning himself in to the Russian embassy, he kept the money and joined the U.S.A. After the war, he married a very beautiful and much sought after New Orleans octoroon and came to Texas. He built his dream house here and claimed five thousand acres of seemingly worthless land and forest. Like everyone else in those days he became a rancher, with cowboys, cattle drives, and everything. In eighteen-seventy-five Gilbert Alfred Yberri, Sr. was born in this cabin. In nineteen-oh-one, Senior built the big house we just passed for our client's mother. In nineteen-oh-three oil was discovered in Batson, and since the Yberris owned most of the land around here, including all the old oil field, they became rich. That was when they hired my grandfather, Scott MacWright, the first, to look after their estate and financial investments. In 1925, our client, Gilbert Yberri, Jr., was born in the big house. He's lived there ever since. Everybody called him Junior until he came home from Korea a genuine war hero, and he has been called Captain ever since."

"Why won't he build a modern home?" asked Sandra.

"It's sort of like the 'old-time religion' with the captain. 'If it was good enough for Grandpa, it's good enough for me,' " replied Scotty, smiling.

"What about the dogs, Scotty? Who's feeding them?"

"Kerry, the Yberri's daughter, lives down the road, and I'm sure she's looking after things. We'll visit her later."

"Scotty, this is unbelievable. These people are tremendously wealthy and live out here in the wilds."

"I told you he was eccentric. Let's go to Batson. You haven't heard the whole story yet."

Chapter 8

Scott drove back to FM RD 770 and turned west toward Batson. Sandra could see a four-way stop sign and a traffic light in the distance. There were a few small houses along the way nestled back among the moss-draped oaks.

"What kind of oaks are these, Scotty? They stay green all the year?"

"They call them pin oaks, Sandra. They produce small acorns. The large, tall oaks without leaves are white oaks and red oaks. The squirrel and deer thrive in here. Over along the bayou there are cypress trees. Moss grows on all these trees—mistletoe, too."

Scott pulled up to the traffic light. There was a small convenience store across the street facing east. To their left facing east was a long wooden structure with a large shelled parking lot filled with cars and pickups of all colors and descriptions. They could hear the singing:

"Amazing grace, how sweet the sound
That saved a wretch like me
I once was lost, but now I'm found
Was blind, but now I see."

"Listen, Scotty, they are singing 'Amazing Grace.' Those people are really vocal in their worship. Does everybody go to church out here? That little convenience store is closed. I bet they are in church."

"You are right on both, Sandra. That's the First Bap-

34

tist Church. Down the road straight ahead about ten miles is the Moss Hill Baptist Church, and up the road to our left about five miles is the Batson Prairie Baptist Church. That church we just passed back there was the Pentecostal church."

"What's the difference, Scotty? The buildings look the same."

"Not a lot, Sandra. They are all fundamentalist. The Pentecostal women don't wear makeup, and they speak in tongues," replied Scotty.

"Speak in tongues?"

"They believe if you are truly saved and possessed by the Holy Spirit, you will burst forth and speak in a foreign or ancient tongue. They call it getting the Holy Ghost."

"Mrs. Gange didn't wear any makeup."

"Then I suspect she is Pentecostal. That is the way you tell the difference."

"How interesting! We could spend a week out here just studying the customs and people. Orient me, Scotty."

Scotty turned right, pulled off the pavement, and stopped.

"This is Old Town, Sandra. There's the U.S. post office, and across the street is the volunteer fire department. Way down the road about a mile this pavement runs into the old Batson Oil field. Would you believe it, Sandra, that along this road in nineteen-oh-three there lived ten thousand people, with sixty saloons, ten bawdyhouses, and there weren't any roads in or out— just wagon trails through the thicket? Many of these houses were built then, and that Baptist church back there was probably the only church for miles."

"I'm getting another history lesson. Did they have a peace officer and a jail?"

"The jail was fifteen miles through the thicket to Kountze by horseback. The people were their own law, and they chained prisoners to some old pine trees down the road a piece. The chain marks are still visible."

"What did the lawyers do?"

"Oh, they were busy buying and selling oil leases and drilling rights. That's how my grandfather got his start. Sour Lake and Saratoga had their boom about the same time Batson did, so he had to move to Kountze, which was the county seat. When they came out with the Model T Ford, he moved to Beaumont, and our family has lived there ever since."

"You finally got around to telling me your family history, Scotty. Now can we get on with this investigation? We are going to feel foolish Tuesday if we walk into that courtroom without any solid witnesses and have to rely on *Whitlock versus Texas*," said Sandra, smiling.

"Okay, Sandra, but the only two witnesses we are going to find this time of day in the old Batson oil field are Buck Rogers, the blind man, and Antoine Como, the old darky. The rest are in church."

"Well, that's a start. Let's go. I'm anxious to start lawyering. I'm in the business of defending the unjustly accused, not wallowing in nostalgia."

36

Chapter 9

Scotty drove through Old Town.

"Scotty, I've decided our client is not the murderer."

"Why, Sandra?"

"You remember that deer with antlers that jumped up behind the barn and ran across the road?"

"Yes!"

"The dogs didn't bark. That means he was a pet. Any hunter that keeps a pet deer around the house doesn't have natural killer instinct."

"What about his heroism in Korea?"

"Out of fear. Anybody will fight if they are pushed far enough."

"How about jealousy, passion, and rage?"

"He would have demonstrated it at a much earlier age."

"The sheriff and the district attorney think he did it."

"They are working on many cases; we have only this one."

"What have you got in mind?"

"You remember the old Roman saying they taught us in law school?"

"'Follow the money trail.'"

"Yes! . . . Please stop when you get to the middle of the oil field and let's get out. With your knowledge of the oil business and my familiarity with the criminal mind, maybe we can figure it out. If it was a local job, then the answer should be here. If it was an outside job, our only connection is American Eastex Oil Company. We've already heard from Mrs. Gange that Terry did not fool around. How long were they married and where did she come from?"

"He married her fifteen years ago. She was working as a cocktail waitress at Lou Ann's. She had a five year old daughter, Kerry Elizabeth, whom the captain adopted and raised like his own. There was no former marriage, and Kerry is the only heir."

"Okay, stop the Jeep and let's start thinking like oil persons."

Scotty stopped the Jeep in the middle of the oil field. They got out, and Sandra started across the field to a slight rise. When they arrived atop the rise, Sandra stopped and they both looked around.

"Stop me if I am wrong, Scotty. I will try to make this quick. Most of these producing fields have three types of wells: natural-flowing, pumping, and gas lift. Let's see. That well I'm pointing to over there with the silver Christmas tree, gauge on top, and a single discharge line with a gate valve is a natural-flowing well. That means the oil comes to the surface under its own pressure.

"That well across yonder with the big electric-driven pump and a single discharge line is a pumping well. You can vary its production by speeding up or slowing the pump. It doesn't have a discharge valve.

"The other type well, which I don't see from here, has gas under pressure entering the well and a discharge line with a control valve.

"The discharge line of about six of these wells connects through a common line to a separator, those long horizontal tanks over there. The gas comes out the top and is pressurized and recycled to the gas lift wells or to a natural gas treater unit. The crude from the separator is pumped to two storage tanks. You can see them all over the oil field.

"You can connect the storage tanks in either series or parallel. The easiest way is to connect them in series. That way you can drain off the water and base sediment from the first tank and with the outflow line fill the second tank with almost pure crude. The discharge line from the second tank connects with the line to the pump station.

"The pumper and gauger comes by and checks all the pumps and valves. He measures the height of the crude in the second tank. He also takes a specimen and spins it down in a centrifuge to measure the suspended base sediment and water. He records this very carefully in his log. He also can open the valve and drain off the water and sediment in the first tank. The gauger has record of the output of the tanks and, if he adds them all together, the whole field. The pump station will measure the flow from the whole field. The gauger's figures and the pump station figures should match. The gauger's records are used to figure the royalties to pay the individual landowners, and the pump station records satisfy the oil company, the Texas Railroad Commission, which assigns the production allotment, and the tax people."

Sandra stopped to get her breath and smiled.

"Bravo, Sandra. Where did you learn all that?"

"I spend every New Year's holiday in the oil field, Scotty. I will tell you later. All that was just background for what I am going to lay on you next."

"Okay, Sandra. I should have brought my note pad."

"This is just a little blue-collar crime, Scotty. Suppose you're just a hardworking gauger and want to steal a little oil without it showing up on your books, and at the same time the pump station gets their same allotment. All the books are perfect. The landowners get their usual royalties, the tax people get their usual payment, and the pump station gets its usual allotment of crude. Assuming you had a buyer for crude in mind, somebody that wanted to pay a little bit less, if they could get away with it—maybe a whole lot less,since it's not costing you anything—how would you go about pulling it off?"

"Sandra, you are talking about 'crude rustling.' That's easy to answer. You would have them drive their tanker trunk up to the tank, suck out the crude, and make it up by increasing the output of the individual wells. Everything would be the same, except you would deplete the reservoir faster. You would have to keep a separate set of books, unless they paid you cash on the spot."

"Suppose you were honest and your boss led you to believe it was a legitimate operation. You would have to keep a separate book for the boss or report to him by telephone the number of tank car loads taken. Suppose everything was by telephone and your boss was paid by cash. Suppose you and your boss were in the cattle business together."

"Sandra, that's a lot of supposing. But we did see Alfred Gange open the gate for that Pakco Limited truck this morning."

"Right! That may be the money trail. Let's go see some witnesses."

Chapter 10

Scotty turned right at the first fork in the road and drove though the old leases. They came to a small frame house nestled in the tree line bordering the old field. It was small, unpainted, and had a tar paper roof through which a stove pipe protruded. There was an outhouse. A mongrel came from under the front porch, on which sat an elderly man wearing dark glasses.

"This is the old Sun Oil lease, Sandra. Mr. Rogers was the maintenance foreman and general caretaker. The captain let him stay on after they abandoned the lease and moved on to bigger and better fields. He has bad cataracts and is almost totally blind," said Scotty.

Sandra and Scotty walked up to the porch. Buck Rogers sat there expectantly, facing them but not seeing.

Finally he spoke.

"You folks are strangers, there are two of you—a woman and a man. You came in a Jeep."

"You do see then," spoke Sandra. "I am Miss Lerner and this is Mr. MacWright. We are representing Mr. Yberri."

"I heard about the captain. No, ma'am, I don't see you. I could tell by the sound."

"How could you tell by the sound?" asked Scotty, getting interested. "You must hear pretty good."

"Driving on that old road, a regular car would have scraped bottom and a pickup would have bounced more and made a lot of racket."

"How did you know we were male and female?"

41

"By the way you closed the doors. That's a Jeep Wagoneer, and the lady got out of the passenger seat."

"Correct on all," said Sandra. "Were you in the field the afternoon of the murder?"

"Yes, ma'am. I was about fifty feet from the main road when the pickup came by."

"Did the sheriff talk with you?"

"Deputy White and Deputy Black came over here on Saturday morning and took my statement. I told them I didn't see a thing, which was the truth. That man might come back and shoot me. I told them I heard two shots about four-thirty P.M. back in the woods. That's all I told them."

"What did you hear, Mr. Rogers?"

"I've had a lot of time to think about it. I can't tell you whether it was a man or a woman, but he drove like a man in a hurry. When he saw me, he slowed down to almost a stop. I could sense he was looking at me. When he finally decided I was blind, he drove off. I keep waiting for that pickup to come back, and when I hear it, I am going out the back door and hide. I got me a place."

"What did it sound like—the pickup?"

"It was about ten years old, by the rattle, and it had twin gutted mufflers or straight tail pipes. Could have been a Ford. Never heard it before and never since."

"Mr. Rogers, is there anything else you can tell us? We want to subpoena you as a witness for the captain. We will send after you. The trial is next week in Woodville," said Sandra.

"That's all I know. You folks like to come in? I don't get many visitors."

"No, we must be leaving. Thank you anyway," spoke up Scotty.

"You're welcome!" called Mr. Rogers as the couple turned and walked back to the Jeep.

Sandra and Scotty were elated.

"Eyewitnesses and character witnesses are notoriously unreliable, Scotty, but the jury loves them. Now we got ourselves an earwitness. I hope he isn't lying just to save the captain. They could cross him up and make us look foolish."

Scotty drove back to the fork and headed down through the old Gulf lease in the direction from which the killer had to come. They slowed when they came to the second fork. They took the road toward Taylor Boudreaux's mobile home, crossed over the wooden bridge, and came to a stop at the locked gate.

"This is as far as we can go, unless you want to crawl through the fence. Here's the gate where they found the fingerprints. The mobile home is around the bend up there by an old warehouse."

"No, Scott, I'll study the photographs. I hate visiting murder scenes. I'm not Perry Mason. I'm sure the sheriff or his deputies will adequately describe it at the trial. We need to keep interviewing prospective witnesses. What's the name of that little stream back there? It sure runs sluggish."

"It's Pine Island Bayou. It joins another tributary about two miles from here and flows into the fish lake. Then it winds its way through the American Eastex field until it crosses FM RD Seven-seventy. It crosses Tex One-oh-five east of Sour Lake and U.S. Sixty-nine at Lumberton. It then empties into the Neches River about ten miles north of Beaumont. I showed it to you this morning."

Chapter 11

Scotty drove back and turned left through the woods on a heavily traveled road.

"This road is in the LouTex field, but the American Eastex fence crosses it about two miles east of here just above the fish lake. There is a cattle guard and a gate there. The east side of the lake is in the AmEastex field. That's where we will find Antoine. Just before we get there the road forks to the right where there are two tank batteries. Mr. Buster Poole has his deer stand there. The road then passes behind a large saltwater reservoir and cuts back toward the dam that holds the lake. There are two pumping wells there that belong to the captain. Close by in the wood line is where Reverend Ebenezer Smythe has a deer stand. Both men were on their deer stands when they heard the shots, and both were there when the deputies came by to investigate on their first trip. They both drive pickups and use shotguns for hunting. The captain lets them hunt there free."

"Will they be there today?" asked Sandra.

"No, the hunting season ended out here yesterday. Very few people in Hardin County hunt on Sunday."

"What do those two men do and where do they live?"

"Mr. Poole and his wife manage the little convenience store you saw at the traffic light. The Reverend Smythe is a retired minister who lives out on the Moss Hill road in a mobile home. He is the father of Willa Gange and grandfather of Willa's children. The late

Taylor Boudreaux was his former son-in-law. He wasn't fond of Taylor," answered Scotty.

"Scotty, let's skip the deer stands and look for Antoine. Will the gate up ahead be closed and locked?"

"Not until five P.M."

Scotty drove over a wooden bridge and slowed down as they passed through the opened gate and over the cattle guard. He stopped and pointed toward two pumping wells. "Sandra, that little shell road leads to those two wells and continues on to the east bank of the fish lake. That's where we will find Antoine. The people from town fish on the west bank."

Sure enough, the elderly Negro, clad in faded blue overalls, khaki shirt, and rubber boots, was sitting on a five-gallon bucket in the shade under a large oak tree. He was using a long cane pole from which a line ran out to a red and white bobber.

"Hello, Antoine!" called Scotty as he and Sandra got out of the Jeep and walked toward the man.

"Hello, missus an' Bossman, yu folks be welcom' to jine me. De's be bitin' pretty good tiday."

They stood and watched him for a minute. He pulled up his line, and the hook was bare. He stood up and opened the lid of the bucket and reached down into the water and pulled out a live crayfish with which he baited his hook. They noticed the bucket was filled with water and contained live fish as well as live bait.

"Is crayfish the best?" asked Sandra, smiling.

"Depends," said Antoine slowly. "Dis time of de year, I want goo, grinnel, an' catfish. I be usin' live crawfish. De spring I be usin' minnow and be catchin' white perch an' bass. De summer I be usin' earthworm and be catchin' goggle-eye perch. I be switchin' bait accordin' what de fishes be wantin'. Dey be showin' me."

45

"Mr. Como, we are lawyers, and we are representing Captain Yberri in the murder trial. May we ask you some questions?" asked Scott.

"Yes, suh! I done told de shurf all I be knowin'."

"Would you tell us?" asked Sandra. "We might send you a subpoena—it's like an invitation—to testify for the captain at the trial."

"Yes, ma'am, jest like on TV. The cap'n, he be in his pickup goin' east at two P.M. Mr. Alfred, he be in his pickup goin' west at five P.M. I hear two shot about two mile west at four-thirty P.M. Mr. Carpenter, he be sittin' his deer stand 'bout quarter mile northeast 'cross de pasture. He be dere at three P.M. an' be left at dark," answered Antoine, smiling. "Dey all drive pickup truck and dey all has twelve gauge shotgun in de back of dey cab jest like de law say."

"Mr. Como, where do you live?" asked Sandra.

"'Bout ten-minute walk east, ma'am, through de wood. I be livin' in a little house 'side de barn. I be fishin' two P.M. an' be feedin' de cow at five P.M."

"Thank you very much, Mr. Como," said Sandra.

They waited for a few minutes and then departed.

"Scotty, I'm getting hungry. It's one P.M.," said Sandra as they got into the Jeep.

"Okay, Sandra, let's drive to New Batson. It's just up the road a piece from the traffic light. We'll come back and talk with the Pooles later."

Chapter 12

They drove back through Old Town and past the traffic light. The church service was over, and in the distance they could see some activity. A few nicely painted frame houses with modern features were scattered along the road. They drove up to a modern shopping mall, which was bordered on the west by a very large and impressive public school with an equally impressive football stadium. Sandra could make out a large sign: BATSON ARMADILLOS STATE CHAMPS 1983. Sandra looked over the shopping mall. Everything seemed closed on Sunday. She recognized K-Mart, Pizza Hut, Dairy Queen, and McDonald's. McDonald's was open and serving! She was hungry.

"McDonald's is open, Scotty. Let's go in," suggested Sandra.

Scott obliged by pulling up to McDonald's. They got in line and eventually ended up in a booth next to a large window giving an excellent view. The church crowd was dispersing, and the customers were clearing out.

"This little shopping mall was constructed just after they built New Batson High across yonder," said Scotty, directing his attention to the school.

"Where do they all come from?" asked Sandra.

"Batson gets all west Hardin County, Sandra. They bus them in. There are several thriving communities down the road from here. Lots of people back in those woods. Oil, ranching, and agriculture. The economic possibilities are limited only by one's imagination. Lots of retirees live out on Batson Prairie."

"Scotty, I spent last New Year's in Holmes, Texas, about eight hundred miles northwest of here. The oil and the cattle were the same, but there the comparison stops. They had wide open spaces, scattered little mesquite groves, and jackrabbits. Here you have thick woods, big oak trees with Spanish moss, and armadillos. It's very beautiful."

"It's the rainfall and the rivers, Sandra. There are three large rivers in less than an hour's drive from this very spot."

"Scotty, let's move on. It's the Pooles next and then Kerry."

Chapter 13

The little store did not appear busy but was open. Over the gas pump was a sign:

Unleaded Plus	1.12^9
Unleaded	1.08^9
Unleaded Premium	1.17^9
Diesel	1.00^9

In the window was a sign: **WORMS** $1.00. Scotty and Sandra walked in. A middle-aged lady standing behind the counter smiled a greeting to them as they approached.

"Howdy. What can I do for you folks?" asked Mrs. Poole. "The gas is self-service. You pay cash in advance. We got everything in here but beer and whiskey."

"Thank you," said Sandra, returning the smile. "This is Mr. MacWright, and I am Sandra Lerner. We are lawyers representing Captain Yberri, and we would like to ask you and your husband some questions regarding the murders."

"Excuse my bad manners, ma'am. I am Gertrude Poole, and my husband, Buster, is not here right now. He's out breaking the sabbath squirrel hunting. I can blow the cow horn, and he will come in. He's probably not far."

"Maybe that won't be necessary," said Scotty. "We have the deputy's report of the statement he gave. Do you think he has anything else he might have thought of since they questioned him?"

"No, sir. He was out on that deer stand until dark, and we did not find out about the murders of Terry and Taylor until the next day. Tragic and brutal! Nothing happened like that in the ten years we been here running this little store. They was our good friends, and the captain was always friendly and good to us. He doesn't charge us for parking our little trailer house back there in the woods. Wouldn't think the captain really did it—the murders, I mean."

"Who do you think did it?" Sandra spoke quietly.

"Don't know, ma'am. Could be a stranger. However, with the telephone call, the spent shotgun shells, fingerprints at the gate, it all certainly points to the captain. He ain't got no alibi, and the sheriff ain't got no other suspects that we know about. Sounds pretty scary. If it wasn't the captain, then none of us is safe. A shotgun is a terrible weapon for killing. Blowed Terry's face right off and put a hole right through the center of Taylor's chest. That must have been a bloody mess out there. You shoot a deer at thirty or forty yards with a shotgun, and you break his leg or puncture his lung and he goes down. Usually Buster just takes his knife and cuts the big vein in his throat to finish him off. But with buckshot at six feet, it just blows a hole right through. If I identified the real killer, ma'am, he might just walk through that door and shoot me, too. I wasn't paying much attention to who was driving up and down the road that day, but I sure keep one eye out that door now. Jail might be the safest place to be right now, if it wasn't the captain, I mean."

"Can you remember who drove by?" asked Scotty.

"Just the captain. He came by about one P.M. going toward the oil field. He stopped in and bought some Almost Home oatmeal and raisin cookies and a grape Shasta. Said he was going to his deer lease when he finished checking his wells and gauging the tanks. I don't remember seeing him come in. The kids and fans went by here about that time going to the football game at Sour Lake. The deputies came by here about five or six P.M. looking around, and they came back at nine-thirty P.M., when they found the bodies. The sheriff, the EMS, the Jefferson County investigator all passed the corner going and coming—plus all the buses and the football fans coming back from Sour Lake. We had customers to wait on, and I closed up at eleven P.M. All that plus the usual Friday night traffic. With deer season and all, there is just too many pickups too keep up with them all. Our Armadillos beat their Bobcats, and there was a lot of celebrating going on over at the school and the shopping mall. Just a whole lot of traffic and confusion."

"Mrs. Poole, did Taylor Boudreaux come in here much?" asked Sandra.

"Yes, ma'am. Just about every day. I liked Taylor. He had a real pleasing way with women. Most of the men like him but Alfred Gange. You know Alfred married Taylor's ex-wife, Willa, and they got the house and two kids," replied Mrs. Poole.

"Did Mr. Gange come in, too?" asked Sandra.

"Yes, ma'am. Alfred is a hardworking man, and he got real upset because Taylor stopped paying child support when he married Willa. They met by accident in here one day about a year ago. Alfred told Taylor if he didn't pay child support, he was going to ask Mr. Carpenter to take it out of his paycheck. Taylor laughed and said if Mr. Carpenter did that he would see them both in jail. Then Alfred got mad and threatened to shoot Taylor, but Alfred didn't mean it. You know them Frenchmen have really got bad tempers."

51

"What did Mr. Boudreaux do when Mr. Gange threatened to shoot him?" asked Scotty.

"Well, he looked real mean and looked Alfred right in the eye and said, 'You stole my wife. You stole my house. You stole my kids. You stole my dogs. I'll see you in hell before I pay for your adultery.' Then he turned around and walked out. I don't think Taylor ever spoke to Willa or Alfred after that day, but he had to pass right by in front of their house going to and from work. He wouldn't go to see his kids or dogs either."

"Did Mr. Carpenter ever come in here?" asked Sandra.

"No, ma'am. Mr. Carpenter stayed away from Taylor. They was brother-in-laws. Mr. Carpenter used the gate down there on the Saratoga road when he came out to go hunting or to check on things in the AmEastex field. You know, him and Alfred are in the cattle business together, too. Taylor checked on all the drilling rigs and didn't have anything to do with these local wells."

"Mrs. Poole, do you all own this store? I notice all the stores in New Town are franchise operated and your gasoline is a lot cheaper," asked Sandra.

"No, ma'am, Buster and I sold out about five years ago to some Pakistani businessmen. They gave us a good price, too. Paid cash. Now they handle all the business and keep the books in Houston. All we do is open and close and wait on the customers. They pay us a salary. No charging, no checks, and no credit cards. That way, we keep the overhead low and don't have to charge big prices like they do down there at K-Mart. We don't fool with the sales tax either. They handle that out of their Houston office."

"Who supplies your gasoline?" asked Sandra.

"Same people. They have a refinery over there in

Houston. When their gasoline truck gets empty they just go by the field down there and fill up with crude and take it back to the refinery. Saves them an extra trip. Those people are real smart for foreigners. They come by here about once a year and bring their wives with them in a big airport limousine. You know, they are allowed four wives apiece. They wear them veils on their faces and wrap their bodies in shawls."

"Thank you, Mrs. Poole," said Scotty. "I'm sorry we missed Mr. Poole. Do you think he will appear at the trial? I mean, is the sheriff going to call him as a witness?"

"Yes, sir, the sheriff has done told him to be ready to go to Woodville Tuesday morning and just tell the truth," said Mrs. Poole.

"Mrs. Poole, may we subpoena you as a witness for the captain? He's been so good to you," said Sandra.

"Yes, ma'am, Buster and I are forever indebted to the captain, and anything I can do to help is fine with me. I can close down this little store and go to Woodville with him. We only call it a convenience store. The customers will wait; nobody gets real impatient out here."

Chapter 14

Kerry Elizabeth Cuvillier Yberri Fontenot was a lightly tanned, beautiful, and outspoken young woman. Her countenance exuded self-confidence and outdoor ruggedness. She knew her jobs, and hard work was her pleasure. At twenty years old she was a mother of two, housewife, oil person, rancher, and farmer.

"You folks get out and have a seat in the swing here. I'll get us some coffee. We drink ours black, but we've got cream and sugar, if you want it. The kids are sleeping, my husband is off working on a drilling rig in the Gulf, and there's just me and the dog."

The house was a white frame with large windows and a big front porch that had a swing and several rocking chairs. It was back in the tree line on the Moss Hill road about a mile north of the traffic light. A shell road ran up to the large barn and garage combination. There was a corral out back, and Sandra could see several horses and cows grazing. A bluetick hound was sleeping under the front porch. They had a chimney that breathed real smoke, but otherwise they had electricity, gas, and indoor plumbing. A large satellite dish was in the front yard. Everything looked clean and neat.

At first glance Kerry looked familiar to Sandra. Maybe she had seen her at Lou Ann's, but then a lot of Frenchwomen had that strange, dark beauty. This one had obviously been raised by a man; she did the work of a man and made no apology.

Scotty and Sandra sat in the swing, and Kerry

returned in a few minutes with a tray containing a drip grind coffeepot and three coffee mugs. There was a bowl of sugar and a spoon.

"I like mine with a little sugar," said Kerry as she poured the coffee.

"So do I," said Sandra, smiling. "I am Sandra Lerner and this is Scott MacWright."

"I'm Kerry Fontenot, the captain's daughter—well, adopted daughter—and I've heard of Mr. MacWright for years. Glad to meet you all. I knew who you were when I saw you coming up the drive. You're my dad's lawyers."

"You're right," said Scotty.

"What happened to my mom and Taylor Boudreaux was horrible and tragic. Mom had a closed-casket funeral. She's buried at Guedry's Cemetery with the rest of the Yberris. There's plenty of space out there for me and Tommy, my husband, and the kids, too, if they want it," replied Kerry.

"Mrs. Fontenot, do you think the captain did it?" asked Sandra.

"Why, no, and nobody else who knows the captain like I do would think so. We got ourselves a homicidal maniac running around here; a professional hit team out of Houston might have done it. In jail is the safest place for the captain to be until this all gets straightened out and you all get the captain acquitted. If you don't get him acquitted, jail is still the safest place until they find out who really did it."

"The sheriff and the district attorney think your father did it, and apparently they don't have any other suspects," said Sandra.

"Oh, what do they know? Somebody made a crank call saying that they shot their wife—from Devers, at

55

that. If the captain had done it, he would not have called a sheriff—and not the Liberty County sheriff," said Kerry.

"Mrs. Fontenot, why was your mother in Taylor Boudreaux's mobile home that day?" asked Sandra quietly, waiting for a reaction.

"Well, you can bet your rear end she wasn't down there playing patty-cake. She and Taylor were on to something." Kerry dropped her voice and looked around to see if they were being overheard. "It's a long story. It sounds fantastic and unbelievable, but it may be true. Somebody shot them. Whoever did it might have just been gunning for Taylor and Mama happened to get in the way. I don't remember her ever going with Taylor Boudreaux anywhere before. He and the captain were good friends. He would come by the house occasionally and have a drink out on the front porch. Mama kept a bottle of Old Taylor whiskey for him. Why, I even kept one for him, too. Taylor was good company, when he was sober."

"Mrs. Fontenot, are you looking after the captain's house and dogs?" asked Sandra.

"I surely am, and I am checking all the wells and gauging the tanks. It costs me three dollars for a baby sitter to come over here and look after my young ones, and LouTex Oil Company pays me two dollars apiece for checking sixty-five wells. That's just money I can't turn down. The captain started taking me around with him when I was five years old. There ain't anything worth knowing in the old oil field that I don't know. One of these years the captain may retire and turn it over to me, but until then I'll just look after everything until he gets out of jail."

"Mrs. Fontenot, where did your mother grow up,

where did you all live, and how did she meet the captain?" asked Sandra.

"I don't know the details. I was five years old when the captain married Mama and brought us to Batson. The captain adopted me as his own. He raised me as a son *and* daughter. He never was married before, and Mama and me was all he had. Mama didn't tell me much. She was reared in an orphanage in New Orleans. 'Terry' was all she knew. She married my real father, last name Cuvillier—that's French—when she was eighteen. We lived in Burris until I was two; then we moved to Hackberry. My father was killed on a drilling rig when I was four. We moved to Beaumont when Mama went to work as a cocktail waitress in Lou Ann's. The captain fell in love with her, married her, and brought us to Batson. Mama always told me that after Burris and Hackberry moving to Batson with the captain was like dying and going to heaven. I don't remember them ever having a quarrel and the captain ever having a harsh word for me in the fifteen years I've been knowing him. They say the captain killed a lot of enemy soldiers in Korea, but I have never seen him even switch a dog. He liked to sit on a deer stand and look off into the woods, but if deer hunting is a crime, everyone in Hardin County is guilty, including the sheriff," answered Kerry.

"Mrs. Fontenot, do you have any photographs of your mother I could see? I'll bet she was beautiful," asked Sandra.

"She was. I gave the only good portrait I had to the reporter from the *Beaumont Gazette,* a lady. She's going to write a feature article, as a human interest story, and print it along with Mama's picture on Tuesday when the trial starts. I've got some snapshots back there somewhere of her with the kids and me. It'll take me awhile to dig them out. They're just little Brownie pictures."

"Thank you. I'd be pleased to see them," said Sandra.

"What do you think your mother and Taylor Boudreaux were suspecting? You said they were on to something?" asked Scott.

"Mr. MacWright, Mama told me not to tell this unless something happened to her. Since you and Miss Lerner are our lawyers, I will have to ask you for your absolute secrecy. If they were wrong, then we could embarrass a lot of innocent people. If they were right, then we might get our heads blown off, too," answered Kerry cautiously.

"We will not tell a soul, Kerry," promised Scotty.

"That's right, Mrs. Fontenot," said Sandra.

"Mama and Taylor Boudreaux thought Alfred Gange was selling crude to Pakco Limited illegally and accepting cash. They were trying to figure out whether it was Alfred by himself, Alfred and Mr. Carpenter together, or Mr. Carpenter keeping all the cash himself and Alfred just following Mr. Carpenter's orders. You know, Mr. Carpenter and Alfred were in the cattle business, and they were making lots of money. Taylor knew that AmEastex's home office didn't know about it. Mr. Carpenter, Taylor's brother-in-law, kept it on a regional level, so Taylor thought," answered Kerry.

"What is so unusual about that?" asked Sandra. "Out west, they call that crude rustling."

"Well, the unusual part is where the money comes from. Taylor traveled a lot and met a lot of people. He washed his clothes in a washateria, ate in truck stops, and bought his gasoline at convenience stores. He said that he had heard from several different pretty reliable sources that the Pakistani businessmen that own Pakco

Limited are using legitimate businesses to launder money they make from selling narcotics," said Kerry.

"Go on," said Sandra, giving Scotty a glance.

"They buy the heroin in Bangkok and smuggle it into the United States. They sell it to members of organized crime for a huge markup. The cash is used to buy up small businesses to launder the money. They bought up all the washaterias, then the convenience stores which sell gasoline and all the truck stops. They bought an independent refinery in Houston to supply gasoline and diesel fuel to their convenience stores and truck stops. Then they started buying crude in the oil fields at a reduced price and using it in their refineries. They get their money back to Pakistan by buying all their wholesale goods and equipment from Pakistan at artificially high prices. That way they send all their money back home and, since their paper profits are low, they avoid American taxes. Most of their business is in cash, and they keep very few records. No records, hence no proof. Taylor was just interested in catching Alfred Gange, and he was trying to get Mama to help him."

"That makes some sense," said Scotty. "He was trying to catch Alfred and Josh Carpenter in something illegal. Of course, American Eastex may have authorized the crude transactions and it's all legitimate."

"Murder is serious," said Sandra. "I would think that Antoine Como's testimony would pretty much eliminate Mr. Carpenter and Alfred Gange as suspects."

"Well, Antoine works for Alfred, and even an old hound dog knows not to bite the hand that feeds him," replied Kerry Fontenot.

"Mrs. Fontenot, we will be needing you as a witness at the trial. Where were you that afternoon?" asked Sandra.

"Miss Lerner, my husband, Tommy, was home, and we went to the football game over in Sour Lake. We didn't get home until around eleven P.M. and by that time they had taken her body to Beaumont. I last saw Mama alive that morning. She looked happy then. It's funny how God can call you when you least expect it. Just like my real daddy," Kerry said sadly.

"What does your husband do when he comes home, besides spending time with you and your children?" asked Sandra.

"He mostly works around the barn and with the animals. We were planning on getting us a big bull and some heifers and getting serious about the cattle business, too. Guess we'll have to put our plans on the back burner until the captain gets out of jail. I'm just one person, you know," said Kerry, smiling.

"Thank you, Mrs. Fontenot. We have certainly enjoyed your coffee and hospitality," said Sandra as she and Scotty rose to leave.

Chapter 15

Louella Guillory was the next witness on their list. She was the clerk at the convenience store in Devers who had identified a picture of Captain Yberri as one of the customers who made the phone call.

As Scotty drove east on U.S. 90, Sandra spoke out.

"Scotty, do you have a picture of yourself with you?"

"Just my driver's license, Sandra. It's a poor likeness. I bet she won't fall for a trick," replied Scotty. He handed her the billfold, and Sandra took out his driver's license.

"It's just a long shot, Scotty. Those deputies know better than give a witness just one photo. They should have showed her several and then let her pick one out— just like in a lineup. They probably have many men fitting the captain's description that stop in here each day. Unless this lady is unusually sharp or attentive, she probably identified the photo just to accommodate them."

Scotty remained in the Jeep, and Sandra walked into the convenience store toward the counter.

In the back of the store sitting on a stool was a young black man. He was laughing and clapping his hands to sound emitting from an elongated high fidelity portable transistor radio that was blasting the atmosphere with rock music of a definite rhythmic beat. A young black girl with a striped T-shirt and snug-fitting jeans was doing a seductive, rhythmic dance with her eyes closed, her lips smiling, and her head nodding slowly up and down to the beat. Sandra guessed it was Louella. She took a bag of Doritos out of the rack and placed it on the counter. Louella continued to dance until her male companion, seeing Sandra, reached down and turned off the music.

Louella came back to earth and walked behind the counter to wait on Sandra. Sandra handed her a $5 bill. Louella rang it up, bagged the Doritos, and handed Sandra the change. Sandra removed Scotty's driver's license from her billfold and handed it to Louella.

"Did you see this man come in here yesterday, please? It was about five P.M.," asked Sandra.

As Louella looked at the picture on the driver's license, Scotty walked up to the counter and held out a $1 bill toward Louella. Louella continued to look at the picture and glanced at Scotty's dollar.

"May I have four quarters for the telephone?" asked Scotty.

Louella took the dollar, hit the "no charge" on the cash register, and handed the four quarters to Scotty while studying the picture in her hand. Scotty took his change and walked out.

"Yes, ma'am. He be by here five P.M. yesterday," answered Louella.

"Are you sure?" said Sandra.

"Yes, ma'am. Lots of men be stoppin' here every day. Some looks just like him," said Louella.

"If you saw him in a crowd do you think you could pick him out?" asked Sandra.

"Oh, yes, ma'am," said Louella.

"Thank you," said Sandra. She picked up her bag of Doritos and joined Scotty in the Jeep.

Chapter 16

"Scotty, I think we have to drive out to the captain's deer stand and try to find Hosea Lopez. He may turn out to be our best witness," said Sandra.

Scotty looked at his watch. It was 3:30 P.M., a little early for Hosea to be feeding the cows. He turned north at Nome and drove to Sour Lake. When he reached the Sunshine Oil pump station he veered to the right on the old highway. It had been abandoned by the county maintenance and was very rough, even for a Jeep.

"Is there anyone else along this road that might have seen the captain or his truck that day?" asked Sandra.

"The captain has to come along this same route to get to his deer stand. About a mile up here on the right back in the wood line is Earl Tipitt's hog farm. A little farther up on the left is a bee farm. Lots of bees. They collect and sell their own honey. I doubt if the deputies talked with these people. They are just like Hosea—difficult to find," said Scotty.

"The deputies probably came looking on a Saturday. This is Sunday. Maybe we can find them home resting. If we see Hosea driving down the road, we'll just go after him," said Sandra, smiling.

The road was really rough, and several times Scotty had to come to a stop and shift into power transmission. He wondered how they traveled it in their pickups.

He spotted Earl Tipitt's mobile home, ovens, and hog pasture back in the trees. He could see Earl stoking the fire under his ovens. A tall cyclone-fenced pasture ex-

63

tended back and surrounded about twenty acres, providing home to several hundred hogs and their young. Earl lived alone and was not well liked by the citizens of the sleepy little community of Sour Lake. The odor was strong and unpleasant. It came from the ovens.

"Mr. Tipitt, what are you cooking?" asked Scotty as they walked up.

Mr. Tipitt kept right on working and answered, "Garbage from the Beaumont restaurants and cafeterias. Law says I have to cook it before I feed it to my hogs."

"Mr. Tipitt, I'm Scott MacWright and this is Miss Sandra Lerner. We are lawyers representing Captain Yberri in the murder trial," said Scott.

"Pleased to meet you all. I seen it reported on the TV. Wondered when somebody would come around to see me."

"The sheriff didn't send somebody?" asked Scotty.

"Nope. People don't like the smell of my cooking."

"Mr. Tipitt, did you see Captain Yberri pass by here on the afternoon of the murders going down to his deer stand?" asked Scott.

"Yep. He passed down here about two-thirty P.M.and came back by just before dark. Just like always, until they put him in jail."

"Mr. Tipitt, does this road go all way through? Could somebody get out of these woods without being seen?"

"Yes, but nobody does. Road too bad, even when it's dry. Little trail comes out behind the old Buddy Jones place on the Saratoga road. I think they got the wrong man. The captain didn't do it," said Mr. Tipitt.

"What makes you say that?" spoke up Sandra. She smelled alibi or perhaps reasonable doubt.

"Been knowing the captain all my life. He is one of the few folks I know that don't look down on me for raising hogs out here in the woods. It's the garbage I cook that smells bad. Hogs are clean and smart. They make good yard pets," said Mr. Tipitt.

"Mr. Tipitt, will you come to Woodville and testify for the captain? We would like to subpoena you for the defense," asked Sandra.

"Yep. I'll have to get up early and work late, but I'll be there. These hogs gotta be fed every day, ma'am."

Sandra and Scotty walked back to the Jeep.

"That seems like a lonely occupation, Scotty. Does he make much money feeding restaurant leftovers to hogs, having to cook it like that?" asked Sandra.

"Mr. Tipitt is a millionaire. Our firm does some work for him. The citizens got up a petition and asked him to move. He told me once that he clears about one hundred thousand dollars a year. His hobby is selecting blue chip stocks. He hardly ever sells," replied Scott.

"Goodness," said Sandra. "Has he ever been married?"

"Twice," said Scotty. "They both went back home after a few weeks. Came from the Philippines. Said they could raise hogs back home."

Chapter 17

They found Hosea standing up in the bed of his beat up truck. He was watching about fifty or more cows eating hay. His technique was to kick out a bale about every twenty yards. The cows always knew what time to expect him. Hosea inspected the stock very closely while they ate. He knew that only a small percentage came on any one day. The rest had gotten their fill of winter grass in the thick woods.

"Hosea Lopez?" asked Scott.

"Si, señor," answered Hosea.

"We are lawyers."

"Si, señor," responded Hosea.

"Did you see a nineteen sixty-eight blue and white Ford pickup sitting down there about a quarter of a mile on November seventeenth?" asked Scott.

"Si, señor," replied Hosea.

"How can you remember the date?" asked Sandra.

"Si, señora. No payday. November tenth payday November seventeenth no payday," replied Hosea.

"We will send you a subpoena and provide transportation for you to go to Woodville to testify for Captain Yberri," said Sandra.

"Si, señora. You send to Mr. Havaard, my boss. I live in barn."

As they walked back to the Jeep, Sandra said to Scotty, "We've got the captain an alibi, if these people are telling the truth. It all seems too easy, Scotty. Do you think he understood what we were saying? The district attorney will certainly discredit him on cross examination. He doesn't wear a watch, and his calendar is payday," asked Sandra.

"I don't know, Sandra. That's for the jury to decide. I once knew a witness who measured time by how long it took to drink a sixpack."

Scotty and Sandra got into the Jeep and started slowly back over the old road. Scotty pulled off at a fence line that ran off into the woods on either side. Sandra noticed that there was a string of beehives, white boxes, to the south and a dirt road winding its way through the woods to the north.

"This is where the captain parks his truck to walk to his deer stand. It's in the woods about a quarter of a mile back there," said Scotty.

"Why doesn't he just drive to it, Scotty?" asked Sandra.

"Scare off the deer. If he shoots a big buck, he would drive back and put it in the truck. This is one of the best hunting areas in Hardin County. Mr. Havaard leases the stands back in here for one thousand dollars a season. The captain is only interested in big bucks. He won't shoot his own deer. Calls them his pets."

"Who owns this land, Scotty?"

"This land here is owned by absentee landlords living in Beaumont. They just own the land and pay the taxes. The Sunshine Oil Company leases the drilling rights and in turn leases the grazing rights to the cattlemen—Mr. Havaard, in this case. Mr. Havaard leases it to the deer hunters, but he puts the deer leases back in an area where they won't shoot his cows. Most of them use shotguns, so it's not so dangerous. Shotguns are only dangerous up to about a hundred yards. Deer rifles like they use in west Texas are dangerous up to six hundred yards or more. We get a few hunting accidents, some of them fatal, every year."

"How about the beehives?" asked Sandra.

"They are owned by an industrious group of beekeepers, Sandra. They put those hives out all over Hardin and Jefferson counties. They have a little factory in Beaumont that puts out honey which is sold all over the country. The landowners and farmers don't charge them to put out their hives. Bees pollinate the crops. Everybody loves bees."

"I am amazed at the way people can make money. All of this requires human effort, though. You just can't sit back and draw a pension and make these businesses pay," said Sandra.

Chapter 18

Scott turned left off Tex 105 at the Pine Island Bayou Country Club Estates.

"This is where Josh Carpenter and all the new rich in Hardin County live, Sandra."

"This surely looks prosperous out here, Scotty."

"You bet! Golf course, country store, stocked lake, wild game—the whole bit."

"The homes are fantastic and their Christmas decorations are extravagant. What will these homes run, Scotty? They all look like they are sitting on two acres," asked Sandra.

"They start at about one hundred thousand dollars. Mr. Carpenter has one of the largest out here. His property cost two hundred and fifty thousand dollars."

"Goodness, all the comforts of gracious living out here in the wilderness, and no taxes, I bet."

"Well, Beaumont is twelve miles away and they have to pay county and school taxes, but you are right; it is less.

"Listen, Sandra, Hardin County is the place to be right now. Most everybody has a septic tank, but these people have their own water and sewage systems. They have the best of both worlds."

Scott turned into the driveway of a very impressive Colonial-style two-story brick home. There was a circular drive out front, and a four-car garage at the side. Adjacent to the driveway and the garage was a swimming pool surrounded by tables and umbrellas. Everything looked expensive. The woods looked clear out in back. She could see a few deer in the distance. As the dogs weren't barking, the deer were probably pets. She saw a column of smoke and followed it guessing it came from a grill.

"Never mind the front doorbell, Scotty. Let's walk around back. They are cooking outside."

Scotty and Sandra walked around to the back, and standing before a grill was a large man wearing Bermuda shorts, tennis shoes, polo shirt, and baseball cap. His back was turned toward them, and he was grilling hamburgers on an open barbecue pit. His wife was seated in one of several wooden lounge chairs surrounding a table.

"Hello!" called Sandra as she and Scotty walked around the house. "May we join you?"

Both Josh Carpenter and Lynette Boudreaux Carpenter turned at once and greeted them with instant smiles. They seemed very comfortable receiving unexpected guests.

"Look, honey," said Mrs. Carpenter. "We have guests."

Mr. Carpenter turned and waved and continued to turn the burgers. "Come on back; the Josh McCarpenter burgers are coming up. You folks are just in time. Pull up a chair."

Mrs. Carpenter rose and offered them chairs, which Sandra and Scotty were happy to take.

"Let me guess. You all are from the church?" said Mrs. Carpenter.

"No, ma'am," said Scotty. "We are lawyers. This is Sandra Lerner, and I am Scott MacWright. We are defending Captain Yberri."

Sandra thought they both stiffened slightly, but it was brief. They never stopped smiling.

"You folks are just in time. Josh here, grilling the hamburgers, is my one and only lawful married husband, and I am Lynette Carpenter—sister of the late Taylor Boudreaux. We hope you get the killer, if that's what you do. Don't we, honey?"

"Yes, dear. Go get the buns and stuff. Dinner is about to be served," said Mr. Carpenter.

"You all please excuse me for a minute; I'll go get the trimmings, and we can sample the specialty of the house. Don't get up, Miss Lerner, I can manage. We gave the maid off Christmas, and we are roughing it," Lynette said sweetly.

Mr. Carpenter began putting the grilled burgers on a serving tray. He stopped at eight. Sandra wondered if they were expecting guests or just enjoyed eating.

"We import the mesquite wood from west Texas. Gives 'em a real good flavor. Hickory is good, too," said Mr. Carpenter.

Mrs. Carpenter returned with a tray of sliced buns, tomatoes, lettuce, and mayonnaise. She had four Diet Pepsis.

"We are half-safe around here. We drink diet drinks with our hamburgers. We are both on a weight-reducing diet," explained Mrs. Carpenter.

Lynette was dark and slender and looked French. Sandra guessed she was about fifty. Josh was a husky, well-tanned, slightly gray-haired man of about sixty.

After they had fixed their hamburgers and were enjoying them, Mr. Carpenter carefully said, "Taylor Boudreaux was my good friend and Lynette's brother. We were both shocked and grieved by his death. Of course, you know I am district superintendent of American Eastex Oil and Taylor was our employee. We were equally stunned to learn that Gil Yberri was arrested for the double murder of Terry Yberri and Taylor. Taylor was very friendly to everyone, except Alfred Gange, for good reasons. Taylor would take a drink occasionally, and he fancied himself somewhat of a ladies' man. I guess you would say he liked the girls—all the girls, especially pretty ones."

"He used to say 'Taylor whiskey' as a greeting," said Lynette. "He and Terry Yberri were just friends. Thank God they were both dressed when the deputies found them. The captain was grieved enough to find her dead— terrible! It would have just been my luck to be shot in the nude, wouldn't it, honey?" said Lynette as she nudged Josh with her foot.

Mr. Carpenter smiled at Lynette and then turned back to Sandra and Scotty. Mrs. Carpenter was clad in a tennis outfit and apparently enjoyed slipping out of her tennis shoes.

"Mr. Carpenter, if the sheriff doesn't call you as a witness, we will have to call you for the defense. May we ask you some questions?" spoke Sandra.

"Certainly, Miss Lerner. As you probably already know, I was on my deer stand in the old Batson field that afternoon, I would say approximately three miles northeast of where the shots were fired at four-thirty P.M. At the time, I thought absolutely nothing of it. I thought it was a hunter. I did not get word of the tragic deaths until about ten P.M., when Alfred Gange called me here at the house," said Mr. Carpenter.

"Mr. Carpenter, what did Taylor Boudreaux do for AmEastex, and what was his usual work schedule?"

"Taylor was a tool pusher. He made daily rounds on all active drilling wells—that is, our exploratory wells.

We call them wildcats. We have twelve at this time. They extend from above Kirbyville on the north to above Vidor on the south. He would start in Kirbyville around eight A.M. and reach Vidor around noon. He crossed the Neches and drove back to Batson in the afternoon. If everything was going well, he'd finish up around two P.M. If things weren't, he would stay on the job as long as it would take. Taylor would call me every day at noon and give me a detailed report of our drilling operations. He was my eyes and ears, so to speak. He was not responsible for the operation of the established fields."

"Did he change his routine or did anything unusual happen the day of his murder?" asked Sandra.

"Yes! He did not call me at noon, and he did not go by the north Vidor rig and went back to Batson early. Unfortunately, I must conclude he went back to meet Terry Yberri," replied Mr. Carpenter slowly.

"What about anything on the rigs? Any personnel problems? We are desperate, Mr. Carpenter. The sheriff has no other suspect than our client," said Sandra.

"I checked our operation reports and time sheet very carefully myself, looking for an explanation, and found none. We had a roughneck walk off the Vidor rig, and that cost us two hours' drilling time, but nothing unusual. We have a pretty high turnover on those drilling crews."

"Mr. Carpenter, what is the driller's name on your north Vidor wildcat?" asked Sandra.

"Claibert LeBlanc. He works days. In fact, he will be working tomorrow, if you would like to talk with him."

"Thank you very much, Mr. Carpenter. We've certainly enjoyed you all's company," said Scotty, rising to go.

Sandra followed.

"You all come back, and we'll have a real party," said Mr. Carpenter.

73

Mrs. Carpenter followed them to the Jeep. "Taylor was my brother, but you folks should know that he had a real weakness for women. Terry Yberri was just his type. Somebody else would have shot him if the captain hadn't. There's such a thing as defending your home and justifiable homicide. I hope you get the captain off. Terry's death was probably an accident. She probably jumped in the way to shield Taylor, thinking the captain would not shoot her. I know it sounds bad coming from his sister, but Taylor deserved to be shot," said Lynette Carpenter.

"Too bad we don't have Mrs. Carpenter on the jury," said Scotty as they drove toward Beaumont.

"I'm tired, Scotty. I've had enough lawyering for one day. Take me back to the motel. I want to take a bath and watch Paul Newman win a malpractice case."

"I didn't know you liked Paul Newman. I saw *The Verdict* two years ago."

"Well, it's either that or watch Sean Connery outwit the whole Russian navy," said Sandra wearily. "I'm going to take your briefcase, but I'll not study its contents until tomorrow night. You said there weren't any surprises."

"Do you still want to drive up to Woodville tomorrow? I'm really enjoying this. It's better than a Boy Scout hike— I mean the woods and all."

"Scotty, I'd talk to you about going into the cattle business, but I think our first stop tomorrow is the north Vidor wildcat and Mr. Claibert LeBlanc."

74

Chapter 19

8 A.M. Monday, January 1, 1990
"Scotty, what does eight-six-one on that green post stand for?" asked Sandra as they drove through Vidor.

"We are eight hundred and sixty-one miles east of El Paso," said Scotty. "We want to get off IH Ten at eight-sixty-four and go south until we see the wildcat. I will show you."

"I've seen a wildcat before," said Sandra. "A year ago today, in Holmes, Texas."

"Not like this one you haven't. They are drilling at thirteen thousand feet. The derrick is as tall as the Empire State Building. This is a deep field. They say it runs from fourteen to fifteen thousand feet and lies under six counties."

"I thought the oil business was slow in Texas right now."

"It is, but wait until the price of crude goes up. Then you will see some real action. There's no shortage of oil here—just a shortage of cheap oil," said Scotty. "It's just like the cattle business. The price of beef goes up, and everybody starts raising cows."

"If you have seen one drilling rig, you've seen them all," said Sandra as they approached the giant rig. They got out of the Jeep.

The driller saw them and walked over. "I'm Claibert LeBlanc. Mr. Carpenter called, and suggested I help you in any way I can," said Mr. LeBlanc.

75

"Thank you. We were wondering if you could tell us anything that would help in the investigation of Taylor Boudreaux's death. We are defense attorneys hired by Captain Gilbert Yberri," said Scotty.

"Taylor didn't show up that morning, and the next day we heard that he was murdered with some woman in his home over in the old Batson field. Taylor liked the gals. No question about that. He would tell the story about Taylor whiskey. It was his favorite."

"What time would Mr. Boudreaux come by?" asked Sandra.

"Usually about eleven A.M., ma'am. It depended on whether things were running smoothly on the other rigs."

"Did you have an employee resign that day?" asked Sandra.

"Yes, ma'am. We fired him, but we turned it in as a resignation so it wouldn't look bad on his record," replied Mr. LeBlanc.

"What were the circumstances leading to his dismissal?"

"It was about noon, ma'am. Jacques just climbed down that ladder up there and announced he was going home to check on his wife. They lived in a little trailer park over in Rose City. I told him I couldn't shut her down, and I ordered him to climb back up the derrick. He just kept walking to his truck, so I fired him. Told him he was through with American Eastex," said Mr. LeBlanc.

"What was his name?" asked Sandra, turning a little pale.

"Jacques LaShute, ma'am. Haven't seen him since. They lived in the Bayou Trailer Park in Rose City between Vidor and Beaumont."

Sandra glanced at Scotty, who was staring up at the rig.

"Thank you, Mr. LeBlanc," said Sandra. "Let's go, Scotty. We need to hurry."

Scotty followed promptly.

"What's the hurry, Sandra?" said Scotty as they pulled off the side road to Rose City. "The trailer park will be there. It was there when we came by an hour ago."

Scotty pulled into the trailer park. He followed Sandra as she walked briskly to the door of the manager's office and knocked. A middle-aged lady of generous proportions opened the door and invited them in.

"We are looking for Jerry and Jacques LaShute," said Sandra.

"I'm sorry, ma'am, but they left on November eighteenth. Don't know where they went. Left in a hurry; forgot their deposit."

"We are lawyers. Could you give us your name? We may need to talk with you again later," said Sandra.

"Clara Benoit, ma'am. We're in the Vidor telephone directory."

"Which way did they turn when they got on IH Ten?" asked Sandra.

"West, ma'am, going toward Beaumont."

"Thank you." Sandra grabbed Scotty's hand and headed for the Jeep.

Scotty followed obediently. "Sandra, what's going on?"

"I'll tell you later. Right now we are looking for one mean Frenchman with a pretty wife that looks a lot like Kerry Fontenot," said Sandra.

Scotty drove back up on IH Ten and headed for Beaumont.

"Scotty, let me pick your brain."

"I'll do my best, Sandra."

"If you were hiding out from the law—or anybody else, for that matter—where would you go, providing you lived in a mobile home and pulled it with a pickup?"

"Anywhere in Hardin County, Sandra."

"Where is the nearest?"

"The nearest is Loeb or Lumberton, I guess. They are just across Pine Island Bayou. We just keep to our right and follow U.S. Sixty-nine until we are over the bridge at Pine Island Bayou. The first road is Pine Island Lake Road. It follows the Bayou all the way out to Pine Island. There must be a half dozen or more roads that run east through Lumberton that dead end way out there in the woods. People don't even know their neighbors. You can get stuck or lost out there," said Scotty. "I've lived in Beaumont all my life, and I get lost in Lumberton."

"We will have to try, Scotty. Take the first road, Pine Island Road, and drive all the way to the end. This Jeep can go anywhere, can't it?"

"It won't float on water, Sandra," said Scotty, smiling.

Scotty crossed over the bridge separating Jefferson from Hardin County. He turned right at Loeb and headed east on Pine Island Road.

"These houses are certainly sitting on high poles. It must flood out here," said Sandra.

"It looks a little bit like Vietnam," said Scotty. "It's for the high water, but also it's to keep the alligators from stealing their pets and kids."

"Is alligator farming a viable business?"

"They grow wild. You just bait a big hook with a rabbit or a chicken. After they get hooked you shoot them in the eye with a twenty-two. They have a hunting season on alligators. You can sell them. They come around in a truck and pay sixty-five dollars a foot. Alligator meat is good. It chews like white breast of chicken and tastes like frog legs. Like everything else, there is some work involved, and you have to own a boat," said Scotty.

"How big do they get?"

"Some of those old bull alligators get twelve feet long. That's about eight hundred dollars to an alligator hunter," replied Scotty.

Scotty slowed down as the houses started thinning out, the road got rougher, the woods looked wilder, and he saw an old wooden bridge up ahead.

"Sandra, some of these people back here don't even have a mailbox. Those that do use Silsbee as a post office. There must be at least six mobile homes with dogs and shotguns at the end of every trail. It's the same everywhere. The deputies out of Kountze won't even come in here after dark," complained Scotty.

"Scotty, you see that trailer house up there on the bank of Pine Island Bayou with the washpot and clothesline?"

"Yes, Sandra."

"Stop the Jeep and walk up there and ask for directions or something. Make like you are lost or you are looking for your sister. All I want you to do is get a good look at their pickup truck."

"Sandra, the husband may shoot me," complained Scotty.

"It'll be for a good cause, Scotty. I promise you," said Sandra.

Scotty reluctantly got out of the Jeep and carefully walked up the trail and stopped about twenty-five yards from the trailer house. A dog barked, but no one came out. He looked at the pickup and came back.

"Well?"

"Sandra, it just looked like a black nineteen-seventy-nine or -eighty Ford pickup to me. Everybody in Hardin County owns a Ford pickup."

"Was there anything unusual about the tail pipe and muffler?" asked Sandra.

"Sandra, half the pickups in Lumberton have twin tail pipes. It's a sign of virility, like the horns on a deer," answered Scott.

"Just the same, it had twin tail pipes?"

"Yes, but you are not going to sway a Tyler County jury with twin tail pipes, Sandra. They will just laugh," replied Scotty.

"Scotty, I've got to establish reasonable doubt. All the sheriff's evidence is circumstantial. We've got to come up with something by Wednesday morning, when we start putting witnesses on the stand."

"Let's go to Tyler County and see the captain. He's had six weeks to think about it. Maybe he's figured it out," said Scotty.

"At last, I'll get to see the notorious captain. I bet he looks like Peter the Great. Scotty, do you think I could check wells and kick hay off the back of a pickup?" asked Sandra, laughing.

"Sandra, you are a defense lawyer. Please don't let your hormone level get higher than your IQ."

Chapter 20

They headed north on U.S. 69. Sandra spoke first.

"Okay, Scotty, I've put this off, but it's time you told me about the opposition and the jury you helped pick."

"The district attorney is Noah Landry. He's an experienced lawyer and handles a jury like a Baptist preacher giving the final invitation before Judgment Day.

"The sheriff is Mart Pate. Born and reared in Hardin County. Was deputy twenty years. Knows this county like the back of his hand. Good man in a tough job. Drugs are the big thing now. His jail is full, and he has to ship his prisoners to Woodville or Jasper.

"The judge you will like. He's John Bevil from Jasper. He is a descendant of the first white man to set foot in Jasper County. He has one fault: he likes to interrupt and tell the court how it was done in the old days. He is tremendously popular up here. He won't take sides. Just a referee."

"What about the jury you picked for me, Scotty?"

"Well, Sandra, the judge did most of the picking."

"What do you mean?"

"First, he had a show of hands of everyone who watched TV or subscribed to the *Beaumont Gazette*. He excused them. That took care of about half the prospects. Then he had a show of hands of everybody that had to go to work and couldn't take off a week. That took care of all the young men. Then he had a show of hands of everyone who owned a shotgun. Everybody raised their hands, so he didn't dismiss anybody else.

"Then the district attorney and I got our chance. The district attorney challenged all the blacks, and I challenged all the women," said Scotty.

"What was left?"

"About fourteen elderly white male retirees. They are experienced jurors. They sit around the courthouse square and play dominoes. They know the law real good, and they all remember *Whitlock versus Texas*," said Scotty.

"Are they familiar with the details of the case? Do they know the captain?"

"Affirmative on both. They have been discussing it for six weeks, while they were playing dominoes. Word of mouth is the quickest way to spread news in these rural areas. These people don't need big-city newspapers or TV."

"Then, Scotty, this is all going to come down to my final argument. Whether I can beat Preacher Landry at his own game."

"That's why I called you, Sandra. It's reading the jury's mind and gut feeling. Remember, in Texas you can get away with murder if the victim really needed killing."

"Scotty, we can't take a chance on *Whitlock versus Texas*. You are paying for a Houston lawyer, and I'm going to defend the captain just like I would in Houston."

"What are you going to do?"

"We have either to produce the real killer or establish reasonable doubt. I'm going for reasonable doubt. It worked for me in Holmes, Texas, and it ought to work in Woodville. They're maybe eight hundred miles apart, but it's still Texas," said Sandra.

"Do you believe in God, Sandra?"

"Goodness, Scotty, what a question. Why do you ask?"

"We just passed a Church of Latter Day Saints back there, and the concept bothers me," said Scotty.

"Scotty, I'm going to give it to you straight, okay?" said Sandra. "If your mind accepts the concept of a Supreme Being and an eternal hereafter, then it doesn't make any difference whether you are Mormon, Moslem, Jewish, or Christian. That concept saves you. How you choose to worship is a matter of upbringing or individual preference."

"You didn't answer my question, Sandra."

"Everybody has to paddle his own canoe, Scotty."

Chapter 21

"Jail is not so bad," said Captain Yberri. "It's the only chance I'll get to read *Texas*. If you all don't get me acquitted, I'll start on *Alaska*."

Captain Yberri was completely bald, about five feet, ten inches, and closely shaven. Sandra thought he smiled and looked like Yul Brynner. There was something extremely masculine about him, and he had the rugged outdoor appearance of an oil man.

He was smiling constantly and making light of his predicament.

"We have equal opportunity catering service around here. Breakfast from Dairy Queen, lunch from the Pickitt House, and supper from McDonald's."

"Captain Yberri, did you take after your grandfather? You look Cossack," asked Sandra, smiling.

"No, ma'am, my grandmother was French. My dad and I took to oil like a duck to water. My grandfather was a great horseman and liked cattle. I guess you'll just have to call me a Russian coon ass, not Cossack."

"Captain Yberri, you have had quite a bit of time to think about the murders. Have you decided who could have done it?" asked Sandra.

"It had to be someone outside my circle of acquaintances. Since I spent so much time in Batson, I had a subconscious awareness of everything going on about me. I made the rounds every day, and I can tell you exactly what everyone was doing at the time of the reported shooting. I believe your investigation will bear that out."

"How about your wife, Terry? Why was she with Taylor Boudreaux?"

"Taylor had it in for Alfred Gange. He enlisted Terry's help in trying to prove that Alfred was stealing crude and selling it to Pakco Limited. Terry approached me on the subject, and I refused to get involved. I was friends with both Taylor and Alfred, and I made it a point to stay out of their squabbles. What their plan was I don't know."

"You don't think they were having a romantic tryst?" asked Sandra.

"Miss Lerner, I have all the fears and self-doubt shared by most men who are fortunate enough to be married to a beautiful and desirable woman, but I don't think Terry would cheat even if she were in love with Taylor. I lived with her for fifteen years, and hopefully I learned something of her character. I have always felt that women are much more sensitive and complex than men. So I guess no man is ever completely sure. My short answer is no."

"Why would anybody—most probably a strange man—want to shoot Terry and then call the Liberty County sheriff?"

"It is very puzzling. If he were local and trying to incriminate me, he would have called the Hardin County sheriff. Even if he were an outsider and didn't know he called the wrong sheriff, it was my wife he shot. Somebody could have paid him to do it, but there is no logical explanation why. A little stolen crude and cash under the table is not enough to justify double homicide. The sheriff's theory, that I went crazy and shot them in a jealous rage and drove to Devers to make a call to throw them off, is the most logical explanation I have heard.

Unfortunately, if he proves it was true, then I will spend the rest of my life in jail."

"Do you want us to hire a private detective?" asked Sandra.

"Miss Lerner, you have a blank check. You spend whatever you think necessary. I would like to find my wife's murderer, much worse than the sheriff. He has many cases that he's working on. We only have this one," answered the captain.

"You don't mind our investigating your business and private life and the intimate details of your wife's personal life?" asked Sandra.

"Miss Lerner, you can investigate anything I've got or anything you think necessary. I hope by now you have concluded that you are talking to an innocent man."

"Captain Yberri, please don't take it wrong. My job is not to judge you or decide whether you are innocent or guilty. The jury will do that. My job is to present the best possible defense and to use my experience and knowledge of the law to get you acquitted or off with the shortest possible jail sentence. That's what a defense lawyer does, whether his client is innocent or guilty. It's like a football game. The offense tries to score, and the defense tries to stop them. If the jury decides against you, then we will appeal to the next higher court, and so on. If we can establish reasonable doubt as to your guilt, then the jury will acquit you. In the eyes of the law you would be innocent."

"Miss Lerner, I like you. You have fire in the old boiler. You and Scott have got my utmost faith. Give old Noah Landry hell. I've voted for him every time, but if he wins this one, I'm not going to vote for him again," said Captain Yberri, smiling.

Chapter 22

"Okay, Scotty let's take the tour and hear the history lesson now. When I come back up here tomorrow, I'm going to be all business."

"Well, Sandra, the town is the easiest. Everything to see centers around the courthouse square. The courthouse was built out of stone about the turn of the century. The stairway leads up to the courtroom on the second floor. The courtroom will seat about two hundred spectators. I doubt if we have much of a crowd. The weather is fine, and these people will have better things to do. There is the usual jury box on the left. They have both jury deliberation room and judge's chamber. There will be a court reporter and a clerk that also serves as bailiff. The district attorney's table will be next to the jury, and our table will be on the spectators' right facing the jury. Ours is the only case scheduled this week."

"Sounds good to me. Where will the jury be when we recess for lunch and breaks?" asked Sandra.

"Probably out there in their little domino recreation building the county built for them. If the weather is sunny, they'll be out under the trees," answered Scott.

"What will the district attorney and judge do during recess?" asked Sandra.

"Probably go play dominoes or swap stories with the jury. They have to run for reelection up here. They won't discuss the case, Sandra. These old fellows take their dominoes seriously."

"Now brief me on the history please."

"This area was settled around eighteen-thirty, Scots-Irish. They crossed the Neches with their wagons, families, slaves, cattle, and dogs about thirteen miles east of here. Took up subsistence farming and raising cattle. As they cleared the land they added cotton. Achieved real prosperity prior to the Civil War. The county government was organized in eighteen-forty. The slaves were freed in eighteen-sixty-five. After that it was subsistence farming, then timber, and subsequently oil. There are four large man-made reservoirs within an hour's drive of here. The recreation is fishing and hunting. It's a dry county. There are many retirees here. That's the short version, Sandra. Do you think I could get a job as tour guide?"

"Excellent, Scotty. Let's go back to Beaumont. I've still got to study those photographs and reports you gave me before I can watch Paul Newman."

"You watched *Red October* last night?"

"You bet. Sean Connery turns me on."

Chapter 23

8:00 A.M., Tuesday January 2, 1990
Scotty and Sandra arrived early and walked up the stairs to the second-floor courtroom. She could see the men playing dominoes out in the county game room. They were laughing and slapping the dominoes on the table. Several clerical offices were off the foyer, and double doors opened into the courtroom. Rows of stained oak benches lined either side of the center aisle. The swinging gate at the bar allowed them to enter the participant areas. *Early American*, thought Sandra. Just like Holmes, Texas.

"Scotty, we are early! Why don't you find us some coffee while I sit here and watch the spectators come in?" suggested Sandra.

"Okay, Sandra. Noah Landry will be here at eight forty-five, and Judge Bevil will walk through that door at eight-fifty. He will go back and put on his robe. The jury will file in at eight fifty-five, and the clerk will call the court to order at nine A.M.. The judge doesn't like long opening statements. Be very brief, and don't make any promises you can't keep. Remember, we have *Whitlock versus Texas* on our side. I will go with you to the judge's chambers and introduce you. Don't worry about Noah seeming gruff. He's got a lot on his mind besides just one case. They are calling nine witnesses. The first two are from Jefferson County, so they can get back. The third is Louella Guillory from Liberty County. They have to take her back. The rest are from Hardin County, so they won't have to rush through those as much," said Scott.

Sandra observed some visitors come in who were definitely not southeast Texas. They were the two Fuentes cousins from Houston with their $600 suits, gold cuff links, and manicured fingernails. They sat down close to the back on her left. Across the room on the right were two gentlemen about fifty-five with dark suits and crewcuts. *Feds*, thought Sandra. Then she noticed two uniformed Department of Public Safety (DPS) officers who were sitting on either side of the aisle. That would be highway patrol and narcotics. She noticed a bright young woman who wore horn-rimmed glasses and a press card but did not have a camera or a note pad. *CIA*, thought Sandra. *We're getting the "full court press." There's more here than just a little passion murder. Surely they didn't come all the way just to see me in action. Where are the cops when you need them?* A few of the local gentry were coming in, too. It appeared that all the local people were familiar with Judge Bevil's habits. *I must not concern myself with the spectators*, thought Sandra. *My job is with the jury.*

A Tyler County deputy escorted Captain Yberri in, dressed in a dark suit and tie and looking quite handsome. He wore a big smile.

"Hello, Sandra. You look ravishing this morning. Maybe we can step out for a little rendezvous when this thing is over. That is, when I'm free—so to speak," said the captain, smiling.

Sandra smiled back. "Captain, I am willing to listen to all honorable propositions, but I know now your daughter was right. It *is* safer for you to be in jail—she was referring to *my* safety, not yours. They want you to look pretty for the jury. No mistreatment of prisoners in Tyler County. When was the last time you wore a suit?"

"My wedding," said Captain Yberri.

Scotty returned with the coffee. A tall lawyer with black-rimmed glasses, black suit, and tie walked up the court aisle carrying a briefcase. He looked like a minister. *That would be Noah Landry*, thought Sandra. Their eyes met. They each nodded. Right behind Noah came a balding gray-haired man of about sixty-five, wearing a loosely fitting tan suit with matching tie. He stopped several times to speak and shake hands with the old-timers. That would be Judge Bevil. She saw the room fill up rapidly. The jury filed in, and the bailiff arrived.

"The judge will see counsels in chambers right now."

Noah Landry got the jump on them, Scotty was right on his heels, and Sandra came in last.

The judge, putting on his robe, said, "Scotty, you introduce us to Miss Lerner."

Scotty obliged. Sandra shook hands with both men. She instantly liked them. She bet they had grandchildren.

"Let's have no procedural errors or take any shortcuts. Nothing that an appellate court can throw out. Miss Lerner, we country boys are slow, so be patient with us. If there is any question, approach the bench. If it's serious, we will come back here and discuss it. I've known the Yberris all my life, and I want the captain to have a fair trial. Don't talk to reporters, stay away from the jurors during the breaks. Okay, let's give a good show."

Chapter 24

Dr. Castillo was Cuban-born, American board-certified, and contract medical examiner for Jefferson, Orange, and Hardin counties. He was middle-aged and spoke excellent English with just a slight Spanish accent. The prosecution's first witness, he patiently read the entire autopsy reports of both Taylor Boudreaux and Terry Yberri. Sandra had read these the previous evening. There was little that would help determine who pulled the trigger. The captain seemed very shaken by the description of Terry Yberri's wounds and the brutality of her demise.

"Dr. Castillo, will you please tell the jury in words that they can understand what killed Taylor Boudreaux and Terry Yberri?" asked Mr. Landry.

"Mr. Taylor Boudreaux was instantly killed by a close range—estimated six-foot-or-so—shotgun wound to the center of his chest. It tore a hole through the entire anterior chest wall, taking the heart and great vessels. The nine double-naught buckshot pellets tore through the chest into the anterior fascial lining of the vertebrae and glanced sideways in either direction into the posterior chest wall, where all pellets were located and accounted for. He had no other pathological medical findings.

"Mrs. Terry Yberri was apparently standing sideways, with her right hand outstretched. The second blast tore off her right hand, her face, and half her head, including the brain. She was killed instantly.

"She was otherwise completely healthy and free of any disease or pathological abnormalities. She did have a surprise finding not previously known. She had a congenital situs inversus and dextrocardia, which means her heart was on the right side, her great vessels were on the right, and her internal abdominal organs were reversed. Hence the name dextrocardia and situs inversus."

"No further questions," answered Mr. Landry.

Sandra rose and posed her first question: "Dr. Castillo, how common is dextrocardia and situs inversus?"

"Very uncommon. Maybe one in a million live births. I have done autopsies for thirty years. This was the second."

"Then it was just an incidental finding."

"Yes, ma'am."

"Dr. Castillo, was Mrs. Yberri premenopausal and fertile?"

"Yes."

"Did you find any sperm in the vagina?"

"No."

"No further questions, Your Honor." Sandra sat down.

The next witness for the prosecution was Justice of the Peace, Precinct #2, Hardin County, the Honorable Zekial Wright. Judge Wright had arrived on the murder scene with Sheriff Pate. It was his duty to determine if death was due to other than natural causes and to order an investigation where necessary.

"Judge Wright, what were the circumstances leading to your investigation of the untimely demise of Mr. Taylor Boudreaux and Mrs. Terry Yberri?" asked Mr. Landry.

"I was called by Sheriff Pate at nine-thirty P.M. He picked me up in his official vehicle, and I accompanied him to the scene of the suspected homicide. On arrival it was my opinion, that they met their deaths by foul play, and I ordered a homicide investigation. As was the customary practice, we radioed Jefferson County Sheriff's Department for Inspector Hebert, their homicide specialist, and a professional crime scene photographer. They came and promptly dusted the mobile home, the interior of Mr. Boudreaux's truck, and the gate for fingerprints. They made the usual photographs, which are available for exhibit. Inspector Hebert forwarded to us the entire report and several copies of each of the photographs. When I received the autopsy report, I filled out the death certificates, which is my usual custom."

"What did you enter as cause of death on the certificates?" asked Mr. Landry.

"Gunshot wound of the chest due to homicide on Mr. Boudreaux's and gunshot wound of the head due to homicide on Mrs. Yberri's."

"No further questions," said Mr. Landry.

Sandra approached Judge Wright. "Judge Wright, when you arrived on the scene had anything been touched inside the mobile home or had anything been moved?"

"No, ma'am."

"After viewing the bodies, how would you say they were positioned?"

"Mr. Boudreaux lay prone, and Mrs. Yberri's head and chest were on top of him. He had apparently fallen forward after rebounding against the sofa and wall, and she had fallen on top of him. Her arm was level with her shoulder, and her forearm was stretched out at about a one-ten-degree angle. The right hand was missing."

"Did it appear to you that Mrs. Yberri may have been trying to stop the gunman?"

"Objection! Calls for a conclusion of the witness," said Mr. Landry.

"Sustained!" ruled Judge Bevil. "We have a homicide expert coming up next, Miss Lerner. In the old days the justice of the peace held an inquest, but things have changed. He just decides who gets investigated and orders an autopsy. The county pays for it."

"Your Honor, Judge Wright is a mature and experienced investigator. The defense thinks his opinion would be very valuable," said Sandra.

"Objection sustained, Miss Lerner. Let's play by the rules."

Chapter 25

Inspector Raymond Hebert was a light skinned Negro, forty-five, trim, and dressed in the traditional gray-tan uniform, complete with western boots and hat. He spoke excellent English with no accent and wore the insignia of the Jefferson County Sheriff's Department. He was sworn in. The district attorney quickly established his expertise. His credentials included a college degree in law enforcement, graduation from the DPS academy in Austin, attendance at numerous seminars, four years of active U.S. Army duty in the Military Police—Vietnam veteran—and lieutenant colonel in the U.S. Army Reserve. He produced the crime scene photographs, which Mr. Landry entered as state's evidence. The photographs were quickly passed to judge and jury. The defense had no objection. Sandra had studied them the night before and was satisfied they were the originals. Inspector Hebert very rapidly described the gory scene, while flashing photochrome duplicates on a large screen from a hand-controlled 35mm film projector. He included pictures of the wall behind the bodies, the missing anatomy, and all eighteen shots. He briefly described the method used for obtaining fingerprints on the interior of the mobile home, Taylor's pickup, and the gate. He was complete, concise, and professional. After completing his lecture, he took his seat in the witness chair.

"Thank you, Inspector Hebert," said Mr. Landry. "Those pictures were pretty bad, weren't they. Oh, not the photography, what they portrayed, I mean."

"Yes, sir. A shotgun at short range is a terrible weapon," replied Inspector Hebert.

"Inspector Hebert, were you able to conclude, after studying the position of the bodies, the furniture arrangement, and the trajectory of the pellets, who was shot first and whether Mrs. Yberri was an intended target?"

"Yes, sir. Mr. Boudreaux was seated on a couch behind the table facing the door. Mrs. Yberri was seated across from him and slightly to his right. Mr. Boudreaux caught the first shot in his chest as he was rising. The momentum carried him backward against the wall, from which he rebounded forward against the table, collapsing it. He then fell forward on the floor. There was no evidence of seizure activity or flailing. Death was instantaneous.

"Mrs. Yberri jumped up and wheeled to her right. Her momentum and balance carried her into the line of fire. The second shot, which must have followed the first by about two seconds, severed her hand at the wrist and caught the right side of her head anterior to the ears, taking that portion of her head off. The severed parts stuck to the wall and fell by their own weight onto the couch. The momentum of her body carried her forward, landing on Mr. Boudreaux's body. There was no evidence of seizure activity or flailing. Death was instantaneous.

"It is my opinion that Mrs. Yberri never saw her assailant and that the murderer only saw the back of Mrs. Yberri as he came through the door. This would lead me to conclude that Mr. Boudreaux was the intended victim. Whether Mrs. Yberri was an intentional victim is open to speculation."

"Inspector Hebert, will you briefly summarize again the fingerprint investigation?" requested Mr. Landry.

"There were no third-party fingerprints on the door

or in the interior of the mobile home and truck. We found the fingerprints of Alfred Gange and Taylor Boudreaux on the gate next to the lock. The lock was a Master and was too rough for prints. We found the palm and fingerprints of Gilbert Yberri on the top of the gate about three feet from the lock. It was his left hand. No other fingerprints were found."

"Thank you, Inspector Hebert. No further questions, Your Honor," said Mr. Landry.

Sandra said, "Inspector Hebert, could you rule out accidental—?"

"Objection, witness has answered the question," said Mr. Landry.

"Sustained," ruled Judge Bevil. "Counsel will approach the bench."

Sandra and Noah Landry walked to the judge's left on the side away from the jury.

Judge Bevil whispered, "Miss Lerner, every man sitting on the jury has killed deer with shotguns, using double-ought buckshot, and everyone remembers *Whitlock versus State of Texas* in Beaumont in nineteen forty-eight. We will not use the term 'accidental' in cross-examination of the state's witnesses. If you want to speculate in your summation, you are free to do so."

"Thank you, Your Honor," said Mr. Landry.

"Thanks," said Sandra.

Judge Bevil smiled and said, "Let's move on, Miss Lerner; we have to get these first two witnesses back to Beaumont. They have to work to do."

"Inspector Hebert, did you draw any conclusions as to why you only found one print of Mr. Yberri's hand on the center of the gate?" asked Sandra.

"Objection, calls for speculation on part of the witness," said Mr. Landry.

"Sustained!" Judge Bevil smiled and spoke to the jury. "You gentlemen all know to disregard that question. Erase it from your minds."

Sandra smiled. She had made her point. There were twelve "country lawyers" sitting on the jury, and she was learning the ropes.

"Inspector Hebert, did you examine the spent shells found at the scene of the crime?" asked Sandra, smiling.

"That's the sheriff's job, ma'am. I'm just a specialist," said Inspector Hebert, smiling.

The jury smiled and the audience tittered.

"No further questions," said Sandra.

Judge Bevil struck the gavel. "Recess for coffee. Everybody back in their seats in fifteen minutes."

Sandra realized that Louella Guillory was next. After that it would be all Hardin County.

"Captain Yberri, do you think your own mother would recognize you in that suit?"

"Probably not. I'm bald now," said Captain Yberri, smiling.

"What were you wearing when you went deer hunting on that fatal day?" asked Sandra.

"Hunting cap with visor, but I assure you I didn't drive over to Devers."

"All the other hunters wear the same?"

"Yep."

Chapter 26

Louella Guillory was dressed up. She looked very pretty and bright. She had ridden all the way from the little town of Devers in a deputy's car. It was her big day. She looked very confident as she was sworn in and took her place on the witness stand. Just like TV.

"Miss Guillory, were you working at Sonnier's Stop and Gas on U.S. Ninety in Devers, Texas, on the afternoon of November seventeenth, nineteen eighty-nine, at or about five P.M.?" asked Mr. Landry.

"Yes, suh," said Louella.

"Did a hunter come into your establishment and ask for his change in quarters to use the public telephone out front?"

"Yes, suh."

"Do you see him in this courtroom today?"

Louella fixed her eyes on lawyer Scott MacWright. She glanced around briefly and then again fixed her eyes on Scotty, who was sitting between Sandra and Captain Yberri.

"Yes, suh," said Louella confidently.

"Would you stand and point him out please?" said Mr. Noah Landry.

Louella stood up and pointed directly at Scotty, who blushed. Sandra and the captain smiled. Noah turned white, the jury smiled, the judge remained stern, and the spectators tittered.

"Miss Guillory, are you sure you are pointing to the right man?" asked Mr. Landry weakly.

"Yes, suh. That be him."

"Thank you, Miss Guillory. You may sit down and stop pointing now." Mr. Landry turned to the judge and said, "Your Honor, may I approach the bench?"

Sandra got up instantly and followed.

Judge Bevil banged the gavel. "Recess for five minutes; jury will remain seated."

Mr. Landry and Sandra followed Judge Bevil back into his little chamber. They all sat down. Judge Bevil burst out laughing. When he could control himself, Mr. Landry said, "Your Honor, Miss Lerner has been tampering with the state's witness. I could petition the state bar association and have her license revoked."

"Oh, nonsense, Noah. What did you do, Sandra?" asked Judge Bevil, smiling.

"Your Honor, I just showed her Scotty's driver's license. The photograph wasn't even a good likeness."

"Chalk it up to experience, Noah. Let's go back in there with a straight face. Maybe they will have forgotten before election."

Chapter 27

Sheriff Pate was tall, good-natured, and fit everyone's idea of what a county sheriff should look like. He could pass for Matt Dillon on "Gunsmoke." Texans always vote for the biggest white man in the county for sheriff. Sandra liked him immediately. He would get her vote. He was sworn in. He had his ten-gallon hat in hand, and his uniform was complete with freshly polished maroon boots, each displaying a single white star.

"Sheriff Pate, was your department in charge of the investigation of the murders of Taylor Boudreaux and Terry Yberri that occurred at or about four-thirty P.M. on November seventeenth, nineteen eighty-nine?" asked Mr. Landry for the record.

"Yes, sir, we were."

"Would you tell the jury the circumstances leading to that investigation and to the findings and charges that resulted?" requested Mr. Landry.

"My department received a phone call from the dispatcher of the Liberty County Sheriff's Department at four-fifty-five P.M. They had received an anonymous phone call from a male reporting that he had shot his wife north of the old Batson oil field. Our dispatcher radioed Deputies Black and White, who took the call and drove over to Batson to investigate. They looked around and took a statement from two deer hunters out that way and then abandoned the search to take another call. Batson Armadillos were playing the Sour Lake Bobcats that night at Sour Lake. It was Sour Lake's homecoming, and there was a lot going on. At nine P.M. we got a call from Captain Yberri informing us his wife, Terry, was missing. So Deputies Black and White drove back to Batson and picked up Alfred Gange and opened the gate leading to the AmEastex warehouse. They found the bodies, which Alfred Gange identified. On our call, the captain came out and verified the identification. I picked up Judge Wright and joined the investigation. On the recommendation of Judge Wright, we requested expert technical assistance from the Jefferson County Sheriff's Department. We did not discuss the case with Captain Yberri until Deputy White read him his rights. Deputies Black and White took Captain Yberri into Kountze, where they notified Mr. MacWright, who Captain Yberri named as his attorney of record. Judge Wright and I remained with the bodies until Inspector Hebert and the photographer finished their work. Then we had the Hull EMS take them into Beaumont to Dr. Castillo for autopsy and forensic study. I dropped Judge Wright off at his house in Saratoga and returned to Kountze in time to hear Captain Yberri's statement. I contacted the county judge, who authorized the arrest of Captain Yberri on suspicion of murder, the lawful search of the captain's premises, and the initiation of the investigation. Captain Yberri appeared before the county judge the following day and the grand jury the following Monday. He was transferred to the Tyler County jail, because our little jail was full. Captain Yberri waived the right to bail."

"Thank you, Sheriff Pate. Would you describe the type of murder weapon used, the spent shells, and the result of the search of Captain Yberri's home?" requested Mr. Landry.

"The murder weapon had to be a repeating twelve-gauge shotgun, because the spent shells found on the floor against the wall to the right of the door. The spent shells were Peters' brand of Remington's double-ought buckshot, twelve-gauge, two and three-quarter inches, the casings were green, and each would have contained nine pellets. A search of the captain's home the following morning revealed an automatic Remington twelve-gauge shotgun that had recently been fired, and his hunting vest contained double-ought buckshot that was identically matched with the two spent shells recovered at the murder scene."

"Thank you, Sheriff Pate. Did you investigate further the anonymous phone call made to the Liberty County Sheriff's Department?"

"Yes, sir, we checked with the telephone company, and their records revealed that a call was placed to the Liberty County Sheriff's Office from the public phone outside Sonnier's Stop and Gas at four-forty-five P.M."

"Thank you, Sheriff Pate. I have no further questions for the witness at this time, Your Honor. Subject to recall or re-cross."

"Request granted," ruled Judge Bevil. "Defense may cross the witness."

"Sheriff Pate, you are a busy man and have many simultaneous investigations for which you are responsible?" asked Sandra.

"Yes, ma'am," replied Sheriff Pate.

"You stayed right on this one, didn't you?"

"As best I could, ma'am. We had four football games and a statewide drug bust going on that night."

"Did you drive over to Devers Saturday morning or drive out to Captain Yberri's deer stand on the old Sour Lake to Batson highway?" asked Sandra.

"No, ma'am, that part of the investigation was

delegated to Deputies Black and White. I believe Deputy White is to testify next, ma'am."

"Sheriff Pate, what percent of the homes in Hardin County would have a twelve-gauge automatic shotgun?" asked Sandra.

"Almost a hundred percent, ma'am."

"What percentage would use Peters' buckshot?"

"Just about all, ma'am."

"Then that part of your evidence is pretty weak, isn't it?"

"Yes, ma'am, it was the telephone call that we could not explain away. Captain Yberri's wife was killed."

"I understand. A man was arrested and now is in jeopardy of life imprisonment on the basis of one anonymous phone call that was incorrectly placed to the sheriff's office of an adjacent county."

"Sometimes we don't even get that, ma'am."

"What percent of homicides remain unsolved, Sheriff Pate?"

"Twenty-five percent, ma'am. We usually have an eyewitness or get a confession. If there is no obvious clue at the murder scene, no eyewitness, and no confession, then it goes way up."

"What is the most difficult type homicide to solve, Sheriff Pate?"

"Shotgun, ma'am. Double-ought buckshot at close range."

"Would it be fair to say that you could walk up to a man out in the woods during hunting season and shoot him with reasonable expectations of not getting caught?"

"Yes, ma'am," replied Sheriff Pate.

"No further questions, Your Honor. Subject to recall and re-cross," said Sandra.

"Request granted. Why don't we all go out and have ourselves a two-coffee lunch? Let me suggest to you visitors from out of town that the Pickett House out on the Livingston highway serves food just like your grandmother used to make with prompt service and reasonable prices. You can get 'fast food' right down the street."

Judge Bevil banged the gavel. "Court recessed until two P.M."

Sandra jumped up from her seat and rushed to the press bench. She stopped a young woman from the *Beaumont Gazette*.

"Are you Ruth Albright, who wrote the article on Terry Yberri in this morning's paper?"

"Yes, ma'am . . . Miss Lerner."

"Good!" said Sandra. "Please bring the photograph with you tomorrow. I want to subpoena you as witness for the defense, so I can enter the picture as evidence."

"Sure thing, Miss Lerner. I will be thrilled," said Miss Albright happily.

Chapter 28

Sandra wanted to get away from it all. So she walked out of the little courthouse and crossed Bluff Street. She saw a sign over a small store: BUNKIE'S DRESS DESIGN AND SEWING. Sandra saw a smartly dressed manikin in the window and walked in. There were dresses on hangers to her left and a small glass showcase and antique cash register on her right. In the back, she saw a dress form, beside which a small woman stood with pins in her mouth and a tape measure around her neck. Sandra estimated her to be eighty years old.

"Hello," said Sandra. "Are you Bunkie?"

The lady seamstress took the pins out of her mouth and said, "You ordering or just looking?"

"Maybe both. I plan to be here all week. Just sort of resting right now. Do you think you could fit me?" asked Sandra, smiling.

"Lady, you've got a nice trim rear. I could probably fit you with stock up there, if you want to try on some."

"I promise you I will let you fit me Wednesday. How's that?" asked Sandra.

"Cash?"

"Yes, cash," said Sandra. "I swear it."

"Miss Lerner, lawyers don't take oaths; neither do judges. Just the witnesses got to tell the truth."

"So you know me; have you been following the trial?"

"Nope. Saw in the paper where the captain had a female lawyer. Guessed it was you when you walked through the door."

"That's brilliant. How did you know?"

"Know every woman in Tyler County. Make dresses for most of them. Except the young ones; they wear blue jeans from K-Mart until they come in here wanting me to fit them for a wedding. Then it's spare no expense, if Daddy's payin'."

"Why do they call this Bluff Street?" asked Sandra.

"Runs out to Town Bluff. That's where the first settlers came across."

"You must know a lot of history then?"

"Nope. Never bother with the past. It's your soul you got to concern yourself with. The good Lord only put us here for a short time to see who's fittin' to go to heaven. Quit chasing the past. It's the rest of your life and eternity that's important."

"I never thought of it just like that," said Sandra, smiling. "I was taught history helps you understand the present so you won't make mistakes of the past."

"You see that old man sitting down there at the courthouse leaning on his walking stick and smoking his pipe?"

"Yes, ma'am," said Sandra.

"That's my cousin George. He's eighty-seven and has forgotten more history than most. Spent his whole life teaching history. If it's history you want, you talk to George. He can tell you where everybody in Tyler County is buried just by their last name. He can also tell where they went to school and who their kinfolks are."

Chapter 29

Deputy Bryant White was black, a sixth generation Texan from Kountze. He was trim and polished, but slightly disadvantaged since he had been told of Louella's goof. He was anxious to make amends. The bailiff swore him in.

"Deputy White, would you please tell the jury the circumstances of your assignment to the case and your findings? Please relate the facts as you know them," requested Mr. Landry.

"Deputy Black and I were traveling southeast on Tex one-oh-five between Votaw and Thicket when we received a call from the dispatcher to go to north Batson oil field to investigate the possibility of a shooting. That was shortly before five P.M. Some man had called into Liberty County, and they had relayed the message to Hardin County. We drove over to Batson. The American Eastex gate was locked. We drove around and questioned two men in deer stands, Mr. Poole and Reverend Smythe. They denied seeing a woman but admitted to hearing two shots around four-thirty P.M. We didn't give it much thought. Plenty of hunters in the woods. Around nine P.M. we received a call that Captain Yberri had reported his wife missing. We drove back to Batson and picked up Alfred Gange, who keeps the keys to the locks. Then we found the bodies and radioed in. When the sheriff arrived, we left. Saturday morning we went back to Batson to search the captain's house. We took a picture of the captain with a buck deer and wearing a hat over to Devers, and Miss Louella Guillory made the identification of the captain as the man who had made the call. We drove around to the old Sour Lake road where the Captain said he was in a deer stand and couldn't find any witnesses. We drove back to Batson and questioned Mr. Buck Rogers, Mrs. Poole, and Kerry Fontenot. That about completed our formal investigation. We have talked with many informally since, but have come up with nothing new."

"Deputy White, did you find anything in your search of the captain's home?" asked Mr. Landry.

"Yes, sir, they are all here in a bag marked for the identification and properly logged in our evidence room at the county."

"What did you find, Deputy White?"

"We found a twelve-gauge automatic shotgun, a vest with double-ought buckshot that matched up with the spent shells found at the murder scene, and this picture with the captain standing by a twelve-point buck and holding his shotgun."

"Did he have a cap on, Deputy White?"

"Yes, sir."

The audience tittered.

"No further questions, Your Honor, subject to recall," said Mr. Landry.

"No questions, Your Honor," said Sandra. She was eager to get on with it.

Alfred Gange was next. Sandra noticed that the hoods from Houston and the DPS, DEA, FBI, and CIA were all still present. It wasn't Deputy White in whom they were interested.

"Your Honor, may counsel approach the bench?" asked Sandra as she walked forward, followed quietly by Scotty and Mr. Landry. They all huddled to the left side of the judge away from the jury.

"Yes, Miss Lerner?"

"Your Honor, the defense moves that we adjourn to your chambers and have a little back room lawyer-to-lawyer talk."

"There will be no plea bargaining, Judge," said Mr. Landry. "We are going for Murder One on both. There will be no lesser plea."

"Okay, Miss Lerner, this is quite extraordinary."

Judge Bevil struck the gavel. "Court recess for ten minutes. Jury please remain seated."

Sandra was anxious as she followed the judge and two lawyers into the chambers and they were seated. She checked the door. The bailiff was standing guard, and there were no windows or other doors.

"Okay, Miss Lerner, this better not be a stall."

"Gentlemen and Your Honor, that place is crawling with unexpected guests out there. There are two hoods whom I recognize from Houston: the Fuentes. There's a sergeant of the highway patrol, a DPS narcotics investigator, two feds who I guess are DEA and FBI, and a little girl sitting on the press bench who looks like CIA. They have stayed through all your witnesses, and I'm betting they are not interested in a little oil field shooting. They are on to something big. You only have one witness left: Alfred Gange. Please let the defense know what is going on," said Sandra.

The judge looked at Mr. Landry, who shrugged and shook his head.

"We don't know, Sandra. I will call in the sheriff." Judge Bevil went to the door and whispered to the bailiff, and in two minutes Sheriff Pate came in and sat down.

"Sheriff Pate, Miss Lerner thinks the DPS, feds, and

111

some members of organized crime are out there to hear Alfred Gange. What do you know?" asked the judge.

"Not a thing, Judge. They have not officially contacted me or given me any instructions. I saw the two DPS sitting in the back. They are in uniform. The hoods are there, but the rest are undercover. Maybe they just want to know if Alfred will talk under oath or plead the fifth. Surely he would not get on the witness stand and admit to some activity that would be of interest to all those people. The CIA works only overseas."

"Well, they are not out there on vacation," said Sandra.

"Do you think Alfred knows? He might have a heart attack," said Scotty.

"No, Alfred does not suspect anything. He thinks he is going to get up there and tell about locking the gates," said Sheriff Pate.

"My questions will be routine," said Mr. Landry. "We will not call him as a witness. He really adds nothing to the state's case at this point."

Judge Bevil listened to it all and finally spoke. "If we pull Alfred as a witness, that will tip them off that we suspect something. My recommendation is to proceed as previously planned and stay within the facts of this case. A man is on trial for his life. Nothing should be suppressed that has a direct bearing on this case. Sandra will just have to use her good judgment on how far to push it. Mr. Landry and I will have to see that she does not break any of the rules of cross-examination. In the final say, I am responsible for this court—it's my decision."

Chapter 30

Alfred Gange was dressed in khaki shirt and pants. He was well shaven, his hair combed, and his shoes polished. He carried a light sport coat folded on his arm. He was wearing a brown tie. Alfred had been an oil man all his life. He was a good worker, and he was dressed in his Sunday best. He was sworn in.

"Mr. Gange, will you tell the court what your specific duties with American Eastex Oil Company are?" asked Mr. Landry.

"I am a pumper and a gauger. I check all the pumps and wells and gauge the tanks in the American Eastex field at Batson, Texas. I report to Mr. Josh Carpenter, the district field superintendent, in Beaumont, Texas," replied Alfred.

"Do you have any responsibility for the physical security of that field, Mr. Gange?"

"Yes, sir. I close all the gates to the field by five in the afternoon. I start out near Votaw and finish closing the last gate in the north Batson field. I open all the gates in the morning; usually they are all opened by eight A.M. I open them and close them at other times for work-over rigs, trucks, and such that are there on company business before or after those hours."

"Who, besides yourself, has a key or keys to that field, Mr. Gange?"

"Mr. Carpenter and formerly the late Taylor Boudreaux."

"Are the gates closed on weekends or holidays?"

"Yes."

"Mr. Gange, would you tell the court what you did on the day of Friday, November seventeenth, nineteen eighty-nine?"

"All day?"

"Yes."

"Well, Friday morning I got up at five A.M., ate breakfast, and fed the cow in the pasture behind my barn. Then I go open the gates. I start out at the north gate of old Batson field, then finish up in Votaw. I start checking wells and tanks in Votaw and work my way back toward the house. At twelve o'clock I go to the house and eat. I go back to the field and finish gauging the tanks. At four-thirty P.M. I start closing the gates. I start at Votaw and finish up at the gate in old north Batson field. On Friday afternoon of the murders, the gate was closed when I drove by. I know Taylor in there, so I don't stop. My son play football that night in Sour Lake. I go to the house. My wife and I put hay in the pickup and go feed the cow on the Saratoga road. Then I come home, eat supper, and watch TV. At nine-twenty P.M. Deputy Black rang my doorbell. He say go with him to unlock the gate. We go and find Taylor Boudreaux and Mrs. Yberri dead. When the sheriff come, the deputy take me home. I watch TV. and go to bed."

"Thank you, Mr. Gange. Did you hear the shots fired between four and five P.M. on the day of the murder?"

"No, sir. At that time I was in Votaw, and too far away."

"Who else was in the American Eastex Field on the afternoon of the murder besides you and the deceased, Taylor Boudreaux and Terry Yberri?" asked Mr. Landry.

"Mr. Carpenter was on his deer stand about one mile from FM RD Seven-seventy in the woods and about three miles northeast of Taylor Boudreaux's trailer house. Antoine Como lives by barn about one-half mile east of the fish lake. Antoine fish from one P.M. until five P.M. Then go feed the cow. Mr. Carpenter got to deer stand three P.M. and stayed till dark, then went home."

"I have no further questions for the witness, Your Honor," said Mr. Landry.

"Mr. Gange, you are Mr. Carpenter's brother-in-law?" asked Sandra.

"No, ma'am. Mr. Carpenter is married to Taylor Boudreaux's sister. I am married to Taylor Boudreaux's former wife."

"Would you say that you and Mr. Boudreaux were good friends?" asked Sandra.

"Before, yes. Taylor no pay child support, and I get mad. Taylor say I commit adultery and steal his wife, his kid, and his house. We no speak to each other for two year. I see Taylor; I go around," replied Mr. Gange.

"Did you threaten Mr. Boudreaux, Mr. Gange?" asked Sandra.

"I say Taylor no pay child support, I go see Mr. Carpenter and get it out of his paycheck. Taylor say he have me and Mr. Carpenter put in jail. I say I kill him. Frenchman no mean threat like that. They have word for hotheaded Frenchman like that."

"Yes," said Sandra. "Are you in the cattle business with Mr. Carpenter?"

"Mr. Carpenter have cow in the AmEastex Company field. He pay Antoine Como and me to feed his cow. I have my own cow in pasture behind my house. Price of beef good right now. Mr. Carpenter buy more cow."

"Mr. Gange, I was out at Batson Sunday morning and I saw you opening the gate for the Pakco Limited tank truck."

115

"Objection," said Mr. Landry. "Irrelevant."

"I think I will let him answer that. Objection overruled," said Judge Bevil. "Finish your question, Miss Lerner."

"Mr. Carpenter, he say let the truck in and show the tank. I report the barrels they take to Mr. Carpenter. He say run the pumps until level in tank back up."

"Who pays for the crude, Mr. Gange?" asked Sandra.

"All business done in district office. I just open the gate and check the pump and tank."

"Do you read and write, Mr. Gange?" asked Sandra.

"I do the numbers and sign my name. I do not know the letters. My wife, she reads good."

"No further questions," said Sandra.

"Court dismissed until nine A.M. tomorrow," said Judge Bevil, striking the gavel.

Chapter 31

Sandra was awakened at midnight by the phone.

"Hello," she mumbled.

"Miss Lerner, this is Deputy Trahan from the Jefferson County Sheriff's Office. I have orders to take you to Woodville."

Sandra flipped on the light and looked at the clock.

"Whose orders? Is there something wrong with lawyer Scotty MacWright? I am not dressed."

"Can't tell you, ma'am. I'm down here with a man from the FBI. Says we've got to move you now. Those are the sheriff's orders."

"Why don't you come up?"

"Can't, ma'am. The lady at the desk won't let us. Says it's against the rules."

Sandra jumped out of bed and dressed rapidly. She brushed her teeth and threw her belongings into her bag. She was downstairs in ten minutes. A sheriff's deputy and a man with a short crewcut wearing a dark business suit were waiting for her.

"This way, Miss Lerner. I'm to take you to Woodville in my official car and put you up in the Magnolia Motel. There I will officially transfer you to the protective custody of the Tyler County Sheriff's Department."

"Officer, I still don't know why you are doing this. Do I have to read you my rights? I haven't paid my bill, and my car is parked out there."

"Miss Lerner, I'm agent Jonah MacBush of the Federal Bureau of Investigation. This is pretty big. We will take care of your car and bill. Our orders are to move you as quickly and quietly as possible. It's for your own safety and government security," said the man with the crewcut.

They quickly ushered Sandra into the automobile and drove away silently into the night. They headed north on U.S. 69.

When they were halfway to Woodville Sandra asked, "Is my associate, Mr. MacWright, all right?"

"Yes, ma'am. He's under protective surveillance," said Mr. MacBush.

They were not telling her anything. She could stand it no longer. "Alfred Gange?"

"Protective surveillance."

"The judge, the jury, the officers of the court?"

"Fine."

"Mr. MacBush, you have simply got to tell me what is going on. You just can't whisk me off in the middle of the night without explanation. This is the United States of America. I have my constitutional rights. I am in the middle of a murder trial. A man's freedom is at stake. I'm a member of the state bar of Texas and lawyer on record in the District Court of Jasper and Tyler counties. I am defense counsel in the trial of Captain Gilbert Yberri, who is supposed to be one of your national heroes decorated for bravery under fire in Korea."

Sandra saw that her arguments were futile. Both men remained unmoved. She was desperate.

"I pay my taxes. I will call my congressman," stammered Sandra.

When Sandra said "congressman," the FBI man turned around. She finally hit on a magic word.

"Miss Lerner, it's a 'need to know' priority."

"Well, I surely need to know. I am about to die of curiosity," said Sandra.

"Mr. Josh Carpenter was murdered last night. Thirty-eight in the temple."

"Is that all you can tell me?"

"That's all, ma'am."

Chapter 32

Captain Yberri was smartly dressed in his only suit, clean-shaven, and sharp. *If I could only be sure he were telling the truth, he would make a great witness*, thought Sandra.

"Captain Yberri, may we call you Captain or would you prefer Gilbert or perhaps Mr. Yberri?" asked Sandra.

"Captain is fine, ma'am. It's my nickname. I was discharged from the Reserve long ago," replied Gilbert Yberri.

"Maybe I had better use Mr. Yberri. This is all going into a transcript of the trial records."

"Fine, ma'am."

"Mr. Yberri, will you tell the court what you were doing on the afternoon of Friday, November seventeenth, nineteen eighty-nine?"

"Around noon I left my house and went back to the oil field to finish gauging the tanks and checking the wells. I stopped by Poole's and bought a snack to eat on the deer stand. Then I went down in the old field and finished the tanks close to the old saltwater reservoir. There are two pumping wells in there by the fish lake. I got back on the main road and headed east through the American Eastex field. The gates were all open, including Taylor Boudreaux's. I came out on FM RD Seven-seventy, turned east and then south on Tex One-oh-five until I came to the old Sour Lake to Batson highway. I went down that road until I crossed a cattle guard inside Havaard's fence. Then I stopped and walked to my deer stand, where I stayed until dark. I came back on FM RD Seven-seventy. The gates being closed, I went to the house. My wife was fine when I left her at noon, and now she was gone. She did not like football, so I figured she might be looking for me. I called over to Kerry's, my daughter, and they were gone to the football game in Sour Lake. I drove around the old field. The gates were locked on American Eastex, so I came back home and waited. When she did not come in by nine P.M., I called the Hardin County Sheriff's Office and reported her missing. You know the rest by previous testimony."

"Thank you, Mr. Yberri. Did you call the Liberty County Sheriff's Office?"

"No."

"Did you murder your wife and Taylor Boudreaux, Mr. Yberri?"

"Certainly not. The answer is no."

"No further questions, Your Honor," said Sandra.

"The state has no questions, Your Honor," said Mr. Noah Landry.

"The accused may step down, and defense may call its next witness," said Judge Bevil.

Scotty whispered to Sandra, "Aren't you surprised Noah didn't 'cross' the captain?"

"He's smart. He knows the jury," said Sandra.

Kerry Fontenot, the potential heiress to the Yberri fortune, was clad in jeans, T-shirt, and jogging shoes that were new. She had gotten up early to feed the animals and instruct her baby-sitter. She was anxious to get back to Batson to her gauging job with LouTex. Her reunion with the captain had been sweet but brief. They had discussed the kids, the dogs, and the wells. She was sworn in.

"Mrs. Fontenot, when did you last see your mother, Mrs. Terry Yberri, alive?" asked Sandra.

"I'm not sure, Miss Lerner. I wear a watch, but I don't have time to look at it much. I think it was right before noon. I went over there to get a recipe, and she was fine then."

"When did you last see the captain, Mr. Yberri, before they took him to jail?" asked Sandra.

"Probably the day before. He wasn't there when I went over there, and Mama was fixin' dinner."

"Mrs. Fontenot, do you have a good portrait of your mother that we could show the court and enter into evidence? I think we can get it back after the trial."

"I gave it to Miss Albright with the *Beaumont Gazette*. It was in yesterday's paper on the front page. It was about ten years old, but it was the best picture we had of Mama."

"Where was it made, Mrs. Fontenot?"

"Thompson's Photography Shop in Beaumont."

"Mrs. Fontenot, did Mr. Yberri murder your mother and Taylor Boudreaux?"

"Objection. Calls for conclusion of the witness," said Mr. Landry.

"Sustained," said Judge Bevil.

"No further questions," said Sandra.

"State has no questions," said Mr. Landry.

Gertrude Poole was dressed up. She had on a new hat, a new print dress, and new high-heeled shoes. She spoke to the captain; he nodded and smiled.

"Mrs. Poole, what time did the captain come by your store on the day of the murder?"

"One P.M., ma'am. I glanced at the clock when he walked through the door."

"What was he wearing?"

"The usual, ma'am. Oil field clothes, except he had on his hunting cap."

"What did he purchase?"

"Almost Home oatmeal and raisin cookies and grape Shasta in a can."

"Did Captain Yberri say where he was going?"

"Objection! Hearsay," said Mr. Landry.

"Overruled," said Judge Bevil. "Witness may answer the question. Please repeat, Miss Lerner."

"Did Captain Yberri say where he was going?"

"Said he was going hunting when he got off work."

"No further questions," said Sandra.

"State has no questions," said Mr. Landry.

Antoine Como was dressed the same. His clothes were clean, and his boots had been washed. He carried his straw hat in his hands. Apparently the deputies had given him the subpoena in time for him to clean up before they brought him to Woodville.

"Mr. Como, did you see the captain on the day of the murder?"

"De cap'n, he drive by goin' east in his truck 'bout two P.M."

"Mr. Como, where were you when you saw the captain drive by?"

"Fish lake, ma'am."

"No further questions," said Sandra.

"Antoine, do you own a watch?" asked Mr. Landry.

"No, Mr. Bossman," said Antoine.

"How did you know what time the captain drove by in his pickup?" asked Mr. Landry.

"Cause dat's when I be fishin'," answered Antoine.

"No further questions," said Mr. Landry.

Earl Tipitt was dressed in a gray flannel suit. He

123

looked like a Wall Street broker. Sandra wondered who was feeding the hogs.

"Mr. Tipitt, did you see the captain go by your place on the old Batson to Sour Lake highway on the afternoon of November seventeenth, nineteen eighty-nine?"

"Yes, ma'am. He drove by going north at two-thirty P.M. and drove by going south just before dark."

"No further questions," said Sandra.

"No questions," said Mr. Landry.

Hosea Lopez was frightened. He didn't know what was going on. He thought he was being sent back to Mexico. He was dressed the same as he always dressed. When he placed his hand on the Bible, Sandra thought he was going to faint. Apparently he had come in the same car as Antoine.

"Mr. Lopez—"

"Si, señora."

"Wait until I ask the question, Mr. Lopez."

"Si, señora," replied Hosea.

"Mr. Lopez, did you see a blue and white pickup truck sitting on the old Batson to Sour Lake highway just inside Mr. Havaard's fence pointing north at four-thirty P.M. on Friday, November seventeenth, nineteen eighty-nine.?"

"Si, señora."

"No further questions," said Sandra.

"No questions, Your Honor," said Mr. Landry.

"Your Honor, may the defense approach the bench?" asked Sandra.

"Judge will see counsel in chamber. Court recessed for coffee. Bailiff, please bring counsel some coffee. Be back in your seats in thirty minutes," said Judge Bevil as he struck the gavel.

In chambers, Sandra began, "Judge, the defense has shown that the accused was nowhere near the murder scene at the time of its occurrence. We move that the charges be dropped against our client."

Judge Bevil leaned back and smiled at Mr. Landry. "You were right yesterday, Sandra, but you are on shaky grounds today. What do you think, Noah?"

"Well, Judge," said Mr. Landry, smiling, "I think Sandra and Scotty here have done a good job driving all over Batson on Sunday before New Year's and questioning these people. You know and I know and the jury knows that not a one of them wouldn't lie to keep the captain from going to jail. I'd probably lie myself, if I were the captain."

"I think Noah is right. Let's keep going and leave it up to the jury to decide. That's what they are getting paid for," said Judge Bevil.

"Judge, you and Noah are making it hard on me. What do you want me to do, raise Taylor Boudreaux from the dead?"

"You have an eyewitness sitting over there at the table with you smiling at the jury," said Mr. Landry.

"Noah, don't tell me you still believe it after Hosea's testimony. He was right there by the captain when the shooting took place."

"Tell it to the jury, Sandra. Your time will come."

Chapter 33

Ruth Albright lived up to her name. Journalism major, pretty, and bright. The old men on the jury and Judge Bevil all watched her approvingly as she walked to the witness stand.

"Miss Albright, will you please state your name and occupation?" said Sandra.

"I am Ruth Albright, investigative reporter for the *Beaumont Gazette*."

"Are you the author of the feature article that appeared on the front page of the *Beaumont Gazette* yesterday?"

"Objection, Your Honor," said Mr. Landry.

"Overruled," said Judge Bevil. "Continue, Miss Lerner. There will be no quotations from the newspaper or hearsay evidence admitted in this court. Just first-person facts."

"Miss Albright, whose picture did you publish with the article?"

"Objection. Counsel must produce original picture for examination by the court and enter as evidence," said Mr. Landry.

"Sustained. Miss Lerner, the district attorney is right. You must present the original photograph and document its authenticity," said Judge Bevil.

"Your Honor, that's exactly what I am trying to do," said Sandra.

"Objection overruled. Let's get on with it, Miss Lerner."

"Your Honor, you let Mr. Landry show the photographs of the mangled victims to the jury. That did not make them less dead or prove who pulled the trigger."

"Proceed, Miss Lerner."

"Miss Albright, whose picture did you publish?"

"Mrs. Terry Yberri."

"Is it a policy of your newspaper to check the authenticity of a picture that is copied for publication?"

"Yes, ma'am. It's a must because of the liability that might result."

"Did you personally establish the authenticity of said picture?"

"Yes."

"How did you do that, Miss Albright?" asked Sandra.

"The portrait was given to me by Mrs. Kerry Fontenot, Mrs. Yberri's daughter. I took the portrait to Thompson's Photography Shop. They examined the photograph and referred to their stamp on the back. They looked it up in their records and verified that it was a still photograph of Mrs. Terry Yberri taken on October first, nineteen seventy-nine."

"Did your editor accept that?"

"Yes, ma'am."

"Do you have with you the portrait Kerry Fontenot gave you, and which you published in the paper?"

"Yes, I do."

"Would you give it to me please?"

Betty Ruth opened her purse and took out a small four-by-six black and white glossy photograph and handed it to Sandra. Sandra looked at it closely, then turned it over and examined the markings on the back.

"Your Honor, I would like to enter this as Defense Exhibit Number One," said Sandra.

"Your Honor, may counsel approach the bench?" asked Mr. Landry.

"Motion granted."

Sandra, with photograph in hand, followed Mr. Landry to the judge's left side away from the jury.

"Your Honor, I'm not sure what Miss Lerner is trying to do. How will a ten-year-old picture of the deceased possibly help her case?"

"Your Honor, it's the only authenticated photograph of the deceased I could get, except the ones Mr. Landry produced with her face blown off."

"Your Honor, she may be trying to trick us, like she did poor Louella Guillory."

"So that's the burr under the saddle, Noah. I don't see how a little old photograph of a dead woman is going to affect this case."

"I don't either, Judge. But Miss Lerner is a woman, and she is trying to trick us."

"Come on, Noah. Let's let her have her fun. Maybe she can teach us old dogs a few tricks."

Chapter 34

"Sandra, you've lost me. I don't know what you are trying to do," whispered Scotty.

"Don't worry, Scotty. I am out on a limb. But success is like a monkey climbing a flagpole. The higher you get, the more your rear end shows. I'm going after reasonable doubt."

Claibert LeBlanc was an oil man. He left his drilling rig to come to Woodville. He was obviously grieving, but the unexpected and untimely death of his boss didn't keep him from working. When you're operating a multi-million-dollar rig at fourteen-thousand feet, you don't stop for a funeral. An oil company, like an Esprit British regiment, has a soul of its own. He was sworn in.

"Mr. LeBlanc, did you know the deceased, Taylor Boudreaux?" asked Sandra.

"Yes, ma'am. He was a tool pusher with American Eastex Oil Company. Prior to his death, we could expect Taylor to check our rig shortly before noon each day."

"Did anything unusual happen on your drilling rig the day of his murder?" asked Sandra.

"Taylor—I mean Mr. Boudreaux—did not come by."

"Anything else, Mr. LeBlanc? You're under oath."

"I fired one of my employees."

"Objection!" shouted Mr. Landry, obviously upset. "Irrelevant!"

"Sustained," ruled Judge Bevil.

"Your Honor, may I approach the bench?" asked Sandra.

"Court recessed for ten minutes. Witness and jury, keep your seats," said Judge Bevil as he headed for his little chamber.

Noah and Sandra followed closely behind. Scotty, perplexed, remained seated with Captain Yberri.

"Sandra is going to get the hell sued out of us, John. She is going to create a suspect to try to establish reasonable doubt," Mr. Landry began.

"Sandra, trying to put the blame on somebody else is as old as mankind. Adam probably blamed the serpent for the behavior of his children," said Judge Bevil.

"No, Your Honor, he blamed the apple," said Sandra, smiling.

"First that photograph and now an imaginary suspect. John, where is this going to lead us?" said Noah.

"To the real killer, I hope," said Sandra.

Both men looked alarmed for a few minutes. Noah frowned.

"See there, I established reasonable doubt in your minds," said Sandra.

"You hope! Hope springs eternal! Facts, Sandra, that's the only thing you put before a jury. If you want to spin a fairy tale in your summation, that's fine. It won't be the first time a woman has talked her way out of a fix. We have presented the facts, and the only logical suspect is sitting right over there at the table with you grinning every time you pull our tail. I believe that Russian coon ass is enjoying this trial," said Noah, losing his cool.

"Listen, Noah, he can grin if he wants to. He can afford me, and besides, every American is entitled to his day in court, no matter where he came from," said Sandra.

"Ladies and gentlemen! Let's be seated and reason together," said Judge Bevil. "Now, Noah, that's the first time I have ever heard you use such language. Don't jeopardize your eternal soul. Now let's go back to the fundamentals. You, Noah, are supposed to present the state's case, which you did rather well with help from some very able experts. Sandra, you must defend your client with your entire effort while obeying the rules of evidence and the ground rules laid down by the court. I am the referee and trying to protect us from the boogiemen—the justices of the Appellate Court. Now the jury, they have to decide who is lying under oath and who is not and who is guilty and who is not. If they can't decide, we call a mistrial and get a new jury. Now the hardest decision is when to break for lunch. I've made my decision. Sandra, you lead us down your little pathway to professional ruin and if some poor peckerwood sues us for a million dollars for defamation of character, then I will be coming to your house to eat."

"You like soup, Judge?" asked Sandra, smiling.

Judge, followed by counsel, filed back in.

The judge struck the gavel. "Court resumed. You are still under oath, Mr. LeBlanc. Proceed, Sandra."

"Mr. LeBlanc, would you tell the court the specific circumstances and the word-for-word exchange involving the discharge of your employee on the day of the murder?" said Sandra.

"In public, ma'am, word-for-word?" asked Mr. Le-Blanc.

"Objection," said Mr. Landry. "Hearsay."

"Overruled. Ladies and gentlemen of the audience out there—this does not apply to the jury, court officers, and the defendant—if you find profanity offensive, then I suggest you leave now. I am planning on recessing for lunch as soon as counsel has finished with Mr. LeBlanc," said Judge Bevil.

Nobody left.

"You may answer the question so the jury can hear you, Mr. LeBlanc," said Judge Bevil.

Mr. LeBlanc looked down, then looked at the judge, and then looked straight at the jury.

"It's twelve o'clock, and Taylor no come by. Jacques LaShute climb down from the derrick. I say, 'LaShute, you crazy coon ass, get back up that rig. I can't shut her down for you!' He say, 'Fuck you, Claibert. Fuck de rig. I go home to check on my wife.' He keep walking to his truck. I shut de rig down. Follow him. I say, 'You walk off, you fired. Never come back to Eastex again!' He get in his truck and drive off. I never see him again."

"Mr. LeBlanc, what kind of truck did Mr. LaShute have?" asked Sandra.

"Jacques LaShute have seventy-nine Ford pickup—black," said Mr. LeBlanc.

"What kind of exhaust system did his truck have?"

"Jacques had twin tail pipes, no mufflers. Make noise when he start off."

"Thank you, Mr. LeBlanc. No further questions."

"State has no questions for this witness," said Mr. Landry with a disgusted look on his face. Just another day in the oil patch.

Chapter 35

Mr. Buck Rogers was helped in by Deputies Black and White. Deputy White stopped off at the bar while Deputy Black helped Rogers step up on the witness stand and into the chair. The clerk placed his hand on the Holy Bible, and he was sworn in. He held onto his walking stick with both hands. He had on dark glasses to cover his cataracts, which were unsightly.

Mr. Noah Landry stepped around to the judge and whispered. The judge bent over to hear what Mr. Landry was trying to say.

Mr. Rogers announced quite defiantly, "I may be blind, but I hear very well."

Mr. Landry blushed, the judge smiled, and the jury tittered.

"Mr. Rogers, where were you at four-thirty P.M. on the afternoon of November seventeenth, nineteen eighty-nine, the afternoon of the murders?"

"I was about thirty yards from the main road leading out of the old Batson oil field," said Mr. Rogers.

"What were you doing, Mr. Rogers?"

"I was out looking for discarded aluminum cans."

"Do you remember anything unusual?"

"Yes, ma'am. I heard two shots fired about a mile off, almost due north. They were from a shotgun and about two seconds apart. About ten minutes later I heard a pickup coming through the old Gulf lease. The road is bumpy with ruts and curves, and I estimate the pickup was ten years old. After the pickup turned on the main road leading out of the field the driver slowed nearly to a stop. He was watching me. I went about my business looking for cans using my walking stick, and he drove off."

"Did you notice anything peculiar about the sound of his pickup, Mr. Rogers?"

"Yes, ma'am. It was not an ordinary sound, like a tail pipe with muffler. His made a roaring noise when he accelerated. I believe he had twin tail pipes."

"How did you know it was a man, Mr. Rogers?" asked Sandra.

"He drove like a man," answered Mr. Rogers.

"How can you tell the difference?" asked Sandra, glancing at the jury. She noticed one in the back with eyes closed.

"Well, ma'am, a man drives impatient and a woman drives cautious. They usually sit closer to the steering wheel and don't brake as much. The man was impatient and he braked pretty hard when he saw me; then he gunned the motor when he started off. It gave the mufflers a roaring sound."

"Mr. Rogers, where is the jury box in this room?"

"Objection, Your Honor," said Mr. Landry.

"Counsel, please approach the bench. Court recessed for five minutes. All remain seated."

Judge Bevil went to his little chamber. Sandra and Noah followed.

When the door was closed, Judge Bevil whispered, "Don't be a spoilsport, Noah. Let him have his day in court."

They returned to the courtroom.

"You may repeat the question, Miss Lerner."

"Mr. Rogers, where is the jury box in this room?"

"To my right, ma'am."

"How many females on that jury, Mr. Rogers?"

"None, ma'am. There are twelve men. Eleven awake and one asleep."

The jurors looked around and the man with his eyes closed was nudged. The judge smiled and Mr. Landry frowned.

"No further questions, Your Honor," said Sandra.

"State has no questions," said Noah Landry.

Chapter 36

Clara Benoit was Sandra's last hope. It was a relief when she arrived in the Hardin County deputy's car. She was from Orange County, and they really didn't have jurisdiction. It would have been tough if Clara had refused to come. She had that dark, sexy ruggedness that most Frenchwomen have. Clara leaned toward the pleasantly plump side.

"Mrs. Benoit, will you tell the court where you live and what you do?" queried Sandra.

"I am a housewife, and I manage the Bayou Trailer Park in Rose City," answered Clara.

"Where is Rose City?"

"Between Vidor and Beaumont. It's in Orange County."

"Mrs. Benoit, are you acquainted with Mr. Jacques LaShute?"

"Yes, ma'am. He was a former renter of mine. Was with me about a year. Just took off and left without claiming his deposit. Hasn't come back."

"How many vehicles did he have, Mrs. Benoit?"

"Just a mobile trailer that sat on wheels and a beat-up nineteen seventy-nine pickup truck."

"Would you describe the pickup, please?"

"It was black and had twin mufflers or tail pipes that made a lot of noise when he started off. That's the only time I saw him. When he was starting off and when he was coasting in off the freeway."

"Did Mr. LaShute own a dog?"

"Yes, ma'am."

"Did it bark very much?"

"No, ma'am, just when a complete stranger would come up to the door or when he and his wife would start quarreling loud."

"Did that happen very often, Mrs. Benoit?"

"No more than anyone else. Quarreling is just one form of adult recreation around a trailer park. There was one incident I remember, though," added Clara. "Jerry— that's her name—put a bumper sticker on back on the passenger side. That was her side. Said JESUS SAVES. Mr. LaShute, he put a sticker on his side in the back saying SHIT HAPPENS."

"Did Mr. LaShute own a gun?"

"Yes ma'am. Twelve-gauge automatic. Kept it in the rack in the cab of his pickup. Mr. LaShute liked to hunt, just like every man in Orange County."

"Mrs. Benoit, did the LaShutes ever have any guests?"

"Yes. There was this couple they partied with, and then there was Taylor Boudreaux, who came by himself."

"You knew Taylor Boudreaux, Mrs. Benoit?"

"Yes, ma'am. Didn't know he was murdered until the deputies told me today. He stopped coming around when the LaShutes left. Taylor was real friendly. It's hard not to know a man like that. His favorite was Taylor whiskey."

"Mrs. Benoit, do you remember any circumstances or incident or marital quarrel that might have led up to their leaving so abruptly?"

"I wasn't paying much attention. I watch the soap operas on TV. That's enough for me."

"Do you watch the news?"

"No, ma'am. Just the soap operas."

"Do you read the newspaper?"

"Just the *Vidor Weekly*, ma'am. It carries more specials. I suppose I would have learned earlier about Taylor's death if I'd paid attention. But I sort of plan my life around the soap operas. I'm a soap opera junkie."

"Mrs. Benoit, did Mrs. LaShute have any lady friends, a sister, or any family?"

"I don't remember any, ma'am."

"Your Honor, may I approach the bench?" asked Sandra.

"Recess for five minutes. Witness and jury, keep your seats," said Judge Bevil as he headed for chambers.

Sandra and Noah followed.

"Sandra, you are wearing us out. So you established a link with Taylor Boudreaux. From the testimony heard so far, Taylor must have known every woman of French descent from Jasper County to Orange County. That's six counties. Are we going to question every one of them?" asked Judge Bevil.

"Sandra, the reason why I have taken it easy on your witnesses is I don't think any of them are reliable. You've got an illegal alien that can only say, 'Si, señora," and a blind man who has perfected the art of listening. Every man in southeast Texas owns a beat-up pickup truck and hauls around a shotgun. The twin tail pipes won't fly either," said Noah.

"Gentlemen, have you fellows ever played stud poker?"

"Did you bring a deck of cards, Sandra?" asked Judge Bevil.

"Just one, Judge, it's my ace, and now I've got to turn it over. I'm asking you two gentlemen to allow me to do it," said Sandra.

"You are being female on us, Sandra," said Judge Bevil.

"Judge, you said I must use all my effort, and I'm doing my best."

"Before we agree to anything, John, I want to hear what it is," said Mr. Landry.

"Okay, Sandra, Noah is right. Let us peep at your ace."

"I want to show Mrs. Benoit the picture of Terry Yberri."

"Why, Sandra?" asked Noah.

"I want to see if she can identify it."

"There will be no suggestions or leading questions, Sandra," said Judge Bevil.

"Judge, it's the same trick she played on Louella Guillory."

"Let's go along with it, Noah. We've got a good jury, and I'm nearing retirement," said Judge Bevil.

The judge and counsel returned to the courtroom.

"Mrs. Benoit, would you look at a photograph and try to identify it for the court?"

Sandra went over to the clerk's table and picked up Defense Exhibit Number One. She looked at it and then walked over and handed it to Mrs. Benoit.

Clara Benoit looked at the picture closely and then handed it back to Sandra.

"That's Jerry LaShute," said Mrs. Benoit.

The judge, Noah, and the jury chuckled. They all waited for Sandra to say something.

"Mrs. Benoit, is there any question in your mind as to the identity of the person in that photograph?"

"No, ma'am. She looks ten years younger in that picture, but that's her all right. No question in my mind."

Sandra had run out of witnesses. "No further questions, Your Honor," she said.

"State has no questions, Your Honor."

"Defense may call your next witness," said Judge Bevil.

"Defense rests, Your Honor," said Sandra, dejected.

"Court adjourned until nine A.M. tomorrow, when counsel will present summation." Judge Bevil struck his gavel.

Sandra walked back to the defense table and looked at the captain and then at Scotty. She shrugged her shoulders.

"What are you going to do, Sandra?" asked Scotty.

"Scotty, I'm going to Bunkie's and buy me a new dress. I may buy two so I can wash one at night."

Chapter 37

"Gentlemen of the jury, I am going to skip the sentimentality and plea for mercy and review the facts.

"The prosecution has three pieces of evidence on which it has based its case.

"Number One: The spent shells found at the murder scene were just like the ones found in the captain's hunting vest.

"Number Two: There was a single handprint of the captain's on the gate of the drive leading up to Taylor Boudreaux's home.

"Number Three: The anonymous phone call made in another county saying a man had shot his wife and naming the exact spot.

"Now I ask you, is that enough to convict a man of murder in the state of Texas?

"Now the defense has shown that:

"Number One: The killer was in a nineteen-seventy-nine pickup with twin tail pipes. The captain had a nineteen-sixty-eight Ford pickup with a regular muffler.

"Number Two: Two witnesses said they saw the captain going to his deer stand. One said he saw him going and coming from his deer stand, and one said he saw his pickup at the deer lease at the exact time of the murder.

"Number Three: Plenty of men wanted to shoot Taylor Boudreaux. He liked Taylor whiskey. But the one man with the motive, the means, and the opportunity was fired from his job one hour after Taylor failed to come by. He told his boss he was going to check on his wife.

"Number Four: Terry Yberri, who was shot with Taylor Boudreaux, was shown by direct identification of a photograph to look just like the wife of the man who had the motive, the means, and the opportunity.

"Now the only eyewitnesses we have to these murders are either dead or not confessing. I have done everything in my power to establish reasonable doubt in your minds of the captain's guilt. I cannot raise the dead. You all are experienced jurors. In the state of Texas, a man has the right to defend his home and family. I leave the decision up to your good judgment."

The jury smiled, but Sandra could not tell whether they agreed or were just being friendly. She sat down. She was emotionally washed out.

Chapter 38

"Gentlemen and friends, I have known most of you all my life. Now you all are perfectly qualified to judge the facts of this case. Miss Lerner from Houston has summed up the facts of the prosecution's case. The shells were the same, there was a handprint at the scene, and a man anonymously confessed to killing his wife. The wife was Terri Yberri. Taylor Boudreaux was with her.

"That is enough factual evidence to convict a man of murder in Texas and anywhere in the United States. You will have to use your everyday common horse sense as to the reliability of her witnesses. Miss Lerner has spun a fairy tale. Every day in the state of Texas there must be a thousand men walk off the job to go check on their wives. It's almost like a maternity leave, which is perfectly legal.

"The state has presented good, solid factual evidence. Miss Lerner has tried to sway you with witnesses that would misrepresent the truth as they saw or heard it to save the captain.

"The Good Book says: 'Thou shall not bear false witness against thy neighbor.' It doesn't mean that you should lie to save him either.

"Forty years ago in Beaumont, Texas, a man was acquitted for shooting his wife's lover and accidentally shooting her in the process. Gentlemen, it's up to you to bring Texas into the twentieth century. Standards have changed, and morality has taken on a new definition.

"Gilbert Alfred Yberri shot his wife's lover and murdered her in the process in cold blood with the most destructive short-range weapon ever invented. Mr. Yberri is a known killer. To shoot thirty-five men with an automatic rifle and then kill two with a bayonet requires a savagery not common to us ordinary mortals even in the defense of our country. It requires a man who takes delight in killing."

"Objection, Your Honor," said Sandra. "Captain Yberri's war record was perfectly acceptable behavior, and he was awarded one of our country's highest medals for bravery and gallantry under fire," said Sandra.

"Objection sustained. Jury will disregard Mr. Yberri's war record which you already know anyway. Please do not refer to the war record, Mr. Landry."

"Now if you have a pit bull that delights in killing, you either pen him up or destroy him."

"Objection, Your Honor. Captain Yberri is not on trial for capital murder, as you very carefully instructed the jury," said Sandra.

"Objection sustained. Jury, disregard 'destroy him,' " ruled Judge Bevil.

"I am asking you, I am giving you, the opportunity to pen up that known killer who murdered—"

"Objection, Your Honor. 'Known' refers to his war record, which you have already ruled on," said Sandra.

"Objection sustained. Jury, disregard 'known,' " ruled Judge Bevil.

Mr. Landry, now reaching the peak of his delivery, turned with his back to the audience and pointed his long arm and finger directly at Captain Yberri.

"I am asking you—"

The eyes of the judge, the jury, and the audience turned toward a young woman clad in blue jeans, T-shirt, and loafers who was walking down the center aisle

144

looking for a seat. She looked frightened and had been crying. She looked identical to Terry Yberri. The captain turned pale and half rose from his chair as if seeing a ghost. Noah with his back turned was still pointing his finger at Captain Yberri. The jury had ceased to listen to Noah and were watching the lady take her seat in a space left open in the press row. Ruth Albright was pale and had her hand to her mouth. The lady in the picture was identical to this woman. The dead had risen to judge the living.

Sandra had been intently focused on Noah and his choice of words, waiting to object if he got out of line. When Noah stopped in midsentence, and everyone else was looking at the mystery lady, Sandra asked, "Your Honor, may I approach the bench?"

Judge Bevil said, "This is highly irregular, Miss Lerner. Mr. Landry is in the middle of his summation."

Counsel approached the left side of the bench. Noah was a little slower, because he had turned around and discovered at whom everybody was staring.

"What is it, Sandra?" whispered Judge Bevil.

Both men bent over to hear her answer.

"Your Honor, can we have a short recess? The defense would like to reopen and put on a surprise witness," said Sandra.

"This is highly irregular, Judge. That looks like the dead woman," said Noah.

"I am inclined to agree with Mr. Landry, Sandra," said Judge Bevil.

"Judge," said Sandra, "that's Jerry LaShute."

Judge Bevil and Noah Landry looked at each other; then they looked over at Jerry LaShute.

"I see no harm in it, Noah. Can you remember the rest of your summary?"

"It's okay by me. Can we take a recess for coffee while Sandra gets her next witness rehearsed? Taylor Boudreaux may have girlfriends dropping in here all day since the *Gazette* ran that article," said Noah.

Chapter 39

Jacques LaShute awoke and found his little trailer home deserted. His wife had gone and his dog had slipped out to roam. He looked around and spotted a newspaper freshly opened and on the couch. He saw a picture of Jerry on the front page. He had difficulty reading but could make out the words "Woodville, Texas." He put on his pants and boots. Outside he found his pickup missing. He went back inside and grabbed his pocketknife, wallet, and pair of pliers. He took off running down the little dirt road until he reached a hard-surfaced road. He slowed down but maintained a fast walk. About a mile away he could see a line of scattered houses, some of which had cars out front, which he hoped were unlocked.

Chapter 40

Jerry LaShute looked identical in every way to what Sandra imagined Terry Yberri had looked like. Now to prove that Jerry was the object and Terry was the victim of Jacques's rage. Sandra had seen Jacques in action at Lou Ann's, a scene she could never forget. The shooting at Batson had no eyewitness, and she didn't expect Jacques to confess. She might just end up proving they looked alike and be right back where she was after Clara Benoit's identification of the photograph. Perhaps she could get closer to the truth with Jerry's testimony, but establishing reasonable doubt as to Captain Yberri's guilt was the best she could hope for. Murder with no eyewitness and no confession is tough, and plea bargaining is usually the easy way out. If it went to the jury he might be acquitted of Taylor's death and get manslaughter on Terry's. With the jails all full and overflowing he might get out in three years. Shotgun murders are so messy. A .38 caliber to the temple is much neater. Jacques had the motive, the means, and the opportunity. Captain Yberri was a victim of mistaken identity and an anonymous phone call. No wonder a quarter of all murders remained unsolved! Jefferson County alone had thirty murders last year, Sandra had read in the *Beaumont Gazette*. The sheriff had a big job. The district attorney was concerned with many cases. She and Scotty had only this one. Maybe she could "win this one for the 'Gipper.' "

"Mrs. LaShute, were you acquainted with Mrs. Terry Yberri?" asked Sandra.

"No, ma'am," answered Jerry.

"How did you learn of this trial?"

"I saw the picture in yesterday's paper. It looked like me. I read about Taylor Boudreaux and the lady being killed. I felt like she had died for me. Jacques, my husband, was asleep, so I took his truck and came to the trial."

"Were you afraid of your husband, Mrs. LaShute?"

"Yes, ma'am."

"Had your husband ever threatened to kill you?"

"Yes, ma'am."

"When did your husband threaten to kill you?"

"Saturday night at Lou Ann's."

"What were the circumstances in which your husband threatened you? Tell them in your own words."

"Objection. Irrelevant," said Mr. Landry.

"Sustained. Miss Lerner, I fail to see where this line of questioning is taking us."

"Judge Bevil, may counsel approach the bench?"

Sandra, Noah, and the judge again went back into chambers.

"Your Honor, Sandra is trying to pull another one of her tricks. First the misidentified photograph and now a woman that looks like the deceased. She is going to testify that her husband threatened to kill her after having a few drinks in a honkytonk south of Beaumont. Nobody in his right mind would pay attention to it. It probably happens at least a dozen times every Saturday night at Lou Ann's. Her witnesses are nonexistent and if produced would have been in a similar state of inebriation."

"Noah's right, Sandra. Dance hall witnesses are notoriously unreliable."

"She has a reliable witness, Judge."

"Who and where, Sandra?"

"Me."

The judge, Noah, and Sandra filed back into the courtroom. Sandra had just a slight smile. The two older men were frowning.

"Objection overruled. You may continue your questions, Miss Lerner."

"What were the circumstances in which your husband threatened you Saturday night at Lou Ann's?"

"He was dancing with you, and the music stop. Tommy Roget, his friend, was standing by me and bending over smelling the perfume Jacques gave me for Christmas. Jacques, he see Tommy and let go of you and run grab Tommy around the neck with one hand, and shaking his fist in his face with his right hand, he say, 'You goddamned coon ass. You make pass at my wife, and I kill you.' Then he turned to me and he say, 'I kill you, too, if I see such crap as this going on again!' The black deputy make us leave."

"Had your husband been drinking?" asked Sandra.

"Yes, ma'am," replied Jerry.

"Had I been drinking, Mrs. LaShute?"

"No. Jacques jump up and ask you to dance when drinks were served. You did not get to drink your beer."

"Mrs. LaShute, tell the court where I was seated and where I was at the time your husband threatened you."

"You were seated across the table with the black deputy. He got up and whispered in your ear. The band was loud. We all order drinks. When waitress brings drinks, band play new song. Jacques gets up and ask you to dance. When dance over he bring you back to table. He

150

let go your arm and grab Tommy. You were standing by my chair."

"Was the band playing?"

"No."

"Did your husband raise his voice?"

"He scream. He very mad."

"Do you think I heard his threats to you?"

"Objection. Calls for conclusion of the witness," said Mr. Landry.

"Overruled. Go on, Mrs. LaShute," said Judge Bevil wearily.

"Scream very loud. I think you heard him."

"Mrs. LaShute, how was I dressed?"

"You had on blue jeans, high-heeled shoes, a yellow T-shirt said 'Eat More Armadillo,' and wearing heavy makeup."

"Mrs. LaShute, how do you remember all those things? Surely that must have been a traumatic event."

"When I go to dance, I look very closely at women my husband dance with."

"Mrs. LaShute, where were you born?"

"My foster mother say New Orleans. Her name Thibodeaux and I grew up Jerry Thibodeaux."

"Did you know any of your blood relatives?"

"No. I never get birth certificate. In Louisiana you don't need."

"Mrs. LaShute, do you have any birthmarks or scars that might help in identification?"

"Just appendix."

"Which side is your scar on, Mrs. LaShute?"

"It's in the middle. The doctor operate in the middle. They found my appendix on the wrong side."

"Did your doctors tell you the name of your condi-tion?"

"Appendicitis."

"I mean the condition where the appendix is on the wrong side?"

"Yes. It's big, long name, and I forget."

"No further questions, Your Honor," said Sandra.

"State has no questions, Your Honor."

"Miss Lerner, would you like to sum up again?"

"No, Your Honor."

"Prosecution may resume its summary."

Noah Landry again walked before the jury. He looked down and studied his notes. He turned with his back to the audience and pointed his finger directly at Captain Yberri's eyes.

"I am asking you—"

Before Noah could say the next word a loud commotion and a raging "Jerry!" were heard in the foyer outside the little courtroom.

Chapter 41

Jacques LaShute had driven up to the light at the corner of Bluff and U.S. 69. He had looked over and seen his pickup parked in front of the courthouse. He pulled up behind it, stopped, and left the motor running. He opened his pickup and grabbed his shotgun. He ran up the courthouse steps, taking them two at a time. The shotgun was held waist high and pointing straight ahead. Inside the foyer he stopped, looked around, and screamed, "Jerry!" Standing guard at the swinging doors leading to the courtroom were Deputies White and Black. They both turned pale as they looked down the barrel of Jacques's automatic shotgun. At the county judge's window on the right was Ralph Longfellow, sheriff of Tyler County, wearing his "hawg" in open holster. On Jacques's left against the clerk's window was Sheriff Pate wearing his Peacemaker in open holster tied to his thigh with rawhide. Deputies White and Black were unarmed.

Jacques walked toward the door with the gun before him. The sheriffs assumed the firing position, waiting for him to fire the first shot.

Deputy White moved to Jacques's right and circled around to Jacques's side as Jacques stepped forward. Deputy White, who was a former middle linebacker at Kountze High, instinctively assumed the ready position and growled. Jacques kept his eye on White and turned his back on Black. Black, a former wide receiver at Kountze High, instinctively hit Jacques with a crack back block from the rear at the level of the knees. Jacques fell backward over Black, firing his automatic shotgun into the air and blowing a hole through the third floor and roof of the Tyler County Courthouse. White rushed Jacques from the front with a bone-crushing tackle. As he went down, the shotgun slipped from his hands, and Black instantly covered it with his entire body. Sheriff Pate ran up and put his handcuffs on Jacques's right wrist. Sheriff Longfellow put his cuff on Jacques's left wrist. Ruth Albright stepped out the door and took their picture with a flash bulb camera, blinding them all. Jacques tried to get up, but White would not let go until Sheriff Pate reached over and got Sheriff Longfellow's cuffs and cuffed the two together. Then they helped Jacques up. Black took Jacques's shotgun and emptied out one load from the chamber and three loads from the magazine. Then he looked down the barrel, satisfied it was empty, snapped the chamber closed, and pulled the trigger. An audible click assured everybody that the gun was unloaded.

White took his notebook from his back pocket and read: " 'You have the right to remain silent. You may be represented by counsel. If you do not have one, the county will provide you one free. You are warned that anything you say may be repeated in a court of law,' etc."

The four peace officers then marched Jacques off to jail and promptly charged him with disturbing the peace, reckless use of a firearm, and double parking in front of the courthouse.

Chapter 42

Noah finally finished his summation. The judge instructed the jury, explaining to them the three degrees of murder (premeditated, unpremeditated, and manslaughter) and explaining to them that they had to decide on issues of guilt for each murder. He also pointed out if they came back with first degree in both cases the captain would have to serve two consecutive life terms in prison and with good behavior might get out in thirty years. The jury was instructed to retire for deliberation. The bailiff handed the foreman three boxes of dominoes as they went through the door into the adjacent room. The court remained seated while awaiting their deliberation. You could hear the dominoes slapping the table and an occasional laugh.

"How long do you think they will be out, Scotty?" asked Sandra.

"They don't get out in a hurry, Sandra. The latest research on the psychology of the jury system has recommended that playing dominoes allows the jurors to remain objective. Apparently it's the concentration on numbers that keeps them objective," said Scotty.

"What time is it, Scotty?"

"It's near lunch, Sandra."

"How long does it take to play a game of dominoes?"

"I don't know, Sandra. Thirty minutes, I guess. They may play a round robin. That's like a basketball tournament."

"What time do these fellows go feed the cows?"

155

"They're retired, Sandra. Their wives feed the cows."

The jury finally came out and announced the captain was acquitted of all charges of murder. The captain did a Russian dance on the defense table and then introduced Kerry Fontenot to her new aunt, Jerry LaShute. Noah went back to Kountze to feed his cows. Judge Bevil drove by Sam Rayburn Reservoir to get in a little bass fishing before returning to Jasper. Deputies White and Black followed Sheriff Pate back to Kountze to plan a drug bust. Sandra headed to Bunkie's to pick up her dress. Scotty was waiting for her in front of the drugstore to walk her to the motel. Sheriff Longfellow was on the phone at the Tyler County jail trying to find a local lawyer to take Jacques LaShute's case for free. The jury went back out under the trees and resumed their domino games. A little fox terrier christened the courthouse steps.

Chapter 43

Sandra and Scotty walked back to the Magnolia Motel. Sandra said, "Scotty, I really don't think, as a lawyer, I ought to get into the cattle business at this time."

"Why is that, Sandra?"

"Well, by the time you lease up a pasture, fix the fence, dig a pond, buy a bull and some heifers, get their inoculations, and get ready to start, the price of beef will go down, and you are stuck with feeding them in the wintertime."

"You may be right."

"I want to thank you for inviting me up here. Riding around in the woods with you in a Jeep and coming up to Woodville to enjoy their home cooking and southern hospitality is like going on vacation."

"How much you think we ought to charge, Sandra? I will send you your share of the fee."

"Whatever you think is reasonable, Scotty. You were the one who invited me."

"Sandra, I inherited my practice from my father and grandfather. I haven't increased my fees in years. I don't know what to charge. I don't get many murder cases. I'm going to have to leave you now, Sandra, and get back to Beaumont."

"Whatever you think is reasonable is fine with me. What's your big rush?"

"I've got to get back and feed the cows."

About the Author

George W. Barclay, Jr., was born and raised in south-east Texas in the first half of the twentieth century. After stints as a soldier, engineer, and oil industry roustabout, Barclay settled into the field of medicine as a private physician specializing in cardiology.

The author, and his wife Chloeteel, currently reside with their four dogs on a farm in Woodville, Texas.

Printed in the United States
4814

9 780595 000319